8/04
X

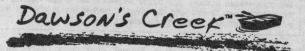

Dawson's Creek™

S U S P E N S E

LIGHTHOUSE LEGEND

Based on the television series "Dawson's Creek"™
Created by Kevin Williamson
Written by Holly Henderson & Liz Tigelaar

POCKET
PULSE

POCKET PULSE
New York   London   Toronto   Sydney   Singapore

This book is a work of fiction. Names, characters, places and incidents are products of the author's imagination or are used fictitiously. Any resemblance to actual events or locales or persons, living or dead, is entirely coincidental.

An *Original* Publication of POCKET BOOKS

 POCKET PULSE, published by
POCKET BOOKS, a division of Simon & Schuster, Inc.
1230 Avenue of the Americas, New York, NY 10020

ISBN: 0-7434-1694-5

First Pocket Pulse printing April 2001

10 9 8 7 6 5 4 3 2 1

POCKET PULSE and colophon are registered trademarks of
Simon & Schuster, Inc.

Cover art by Art Streiber

Printed in the U.S.A.

For Jeanie, Jimmy and Henry—my family —H.H.

For Kate from "Starchild"—L.T.

LIGHTHOUSE
LEGEND

Prologue

September 13, 1852

"Please, Mother!" Mary cried, "don't leave me down here!" Mary held on to her mother's arm, not willing to let it go. Julia pried her arm free of her daughter's strong grasp, giving Mary instead her rag doll for comfort. She kissed Mary's forehead and stumbled up the ladder to the deck.

On deck, her husband Robert and his brothers were struggling. The storm had worsened so quickly that it had become impossible to see. They were using all of their strength just to keep the ship upright. The wooden vessel rode the crest of a wave, then crashed down violently. The boom swung around, knocking Robert to the ground. He slid down the deck of the ship, slamming into the railing. He would have slipped through if Julia had not grabbed hold of his leg. They struggled to pull themselves off the slippery deck. Robert looked as white as a ghost as he rose to his feet. Julia grasped the unsteady boom to keep her balance.

"Are you all right?" Julia yelled. She put her hand over her heart, a mixture of shock and relief. Robert nodded vigorously, unable to mask his fear. "Are we near land?" she screamed above the howling wind.

"I cannot tell," Robert yelled back. "There should be a lightwatchman to guide us, but I've seen no light." Suddenly . . . "What was that?" Robert yelled. "Did you hear that noise?"

Julia looked into the dark night. "It sounded like a foghorn," Julia insisted. "Coming from over there."

Unable to detect their coordinates, Robert put their lives into the hands of fate.

"Maneuver that way!" he urged his crew. They pushed the boom with all their might, as Julia ducked out of the way. Another wave hit as their bow nose-dived toward the water. The ship shook, threatening to break in half from the impact.

"We're taking on more water," Julia yelled as loud as she could.

"Where's Mary?" Robert yelled back, worried.

"Here I am," a small voice answered, barely audible. Mary had climbed the ladder, following her mother above. She stood before them, her bare feet slipping on the watery deck.

"No, Mary!" Julia urged. "Go back below. Now!"

Robert reached for his daughter, just as a wave smashed against the starboard side of the ship. In an instant, water surged over the deck, knocking everyone off their feet. The mast swung free, crashing onto the deck, as the vessel took on even more water. The sea was swirling all around them and they were stuck in the middle, helpless.

Crawling to their feet, Julia and Robert faced their horror together as they found each other's eyes from across the deck. Mary wasn't on deck. Julia raced to the edge of the railing, screaming at the ocean to give back her daughter.

Robert climbed the rail, ready to dive into the water to take her back. He never got a chance. *Queen Mary* careened into the jetty, crashing upon a large cliff beneath the lighthouse. The jagged rocks ripped the ship in half. Crushed upon the rocks and fighting with the sea, the husband and wife weren't strong enough to battle such a force. The sea had dealt the ship her fate. The Breckinridge family disappeared, engulfed in an icy grave.

Mary, too, was engulfed, surrounded by blackness. Able to claw her way to the surface, she opened her mouth. "Mama," she gasped out. A dark wave scooped up her body and carried it, almost as if she were floating above the sea. Then just as quickly, the wave dropped her. She plunged deeper and deeper into the dark water, and another wave closed over her. Death came quickly to Mary Breckinridge. Her eyes stared open, as if she were looking toward what might have been.

1

The Beginning

Joey climbed up the ladder and through Dawson's bedroom window into what appeared to be a picturesque life. His room was quiet except for the murmur of the television. Comfortable in his flannel pajama bottoms and Capeside High T-shirt, Dawson lounged on his bed, watching a movie. Joey slipped off her sandals and reclined beside him. "What are you watching?" she asked.

Dawson, propping his head on his hands, answered, *Summer School*. I'm going for a theme. Last night it was *Summer of 42*. Tomorrow night, *Summer of Fear*."

Resting her chin comfortably on a pillow, Joey mocked, "Considering there are at least a total of twenty-eight motion pictures with the name 'Summer' in their title, you could make this your theme for the entire month." Eyebrow raised in query, Dawson looked at her. Joey, rolling her eyes, admitted, "An informationless tidbit, thanks to the countless movie-night movies you've forced me to endure the last seventeen years of my life." Dawson smiled as he slid closer to Joey on the bed.

Dawson loved Joey like no other person in his life. She was his first friend, first true love, and first real heartbreak. She stood by him when he cried, failed, and succeeded. She even cheered his successes when her life wasn't grand. On a daily basis she pushed him to be stronger, wiser, and more humble. Joey and Dawson had run the gamut of emotions and remained standing strong—together and true. For Dawson, Joey Potter was his soul mate, whether she was ready to admit it or not.

Joey picked up on Dawson's romantic vibe, but, for her, another summer filled with romantic angst was the last thing she wanted or needed. However, her love for Dawson was as deep as his love for her and she couldn't deny that. He knew her better than her own shadow. But, broken promises, financial pressures, and personal pain had left Joey disbelieving in "happy endings" and "ever afters." She needed a summer of mindless fun to recharge and reconnect. She needed to find a part of her that had been lost—her spirit.

Joey hit Dawson with her pillow and teased, "Okay, Dawson, back to pure celluloid with plenty of sun and fun." As Joey and Dawson settled in for the movie, Dawson's bedroom door flew open.

"Sun and fun?" A loud voice vented. "One word I'm having a hate relationship with. And another word that is painfully missing in my life." Joey and Dawson smiled at their crazed and disheveled friend, Pacey, standing in the doorway. His brown hair matted down with sweat and his brightly colored button-down shirt clinging to his chest, he moaned and said, "And if the past week is any indication of what I have to look forward to this summer, I'd rather be back in school." Pacey wiped the sweat from his forehead. "And what's with the heat wave? I'm melting here."

Joey and Dawson glanced over at the window, amused because a light wind was rustling the curtains and blowing a cool breeze into the room. Dawson teased, "Capeside's not having a heat wave, Pace. It's your oversexed hormones with no place to call home."

As Joey laughed at Dawson's joke, Pacey walked over to the bed and plopped down. He smiled at the truth. "Maybe. But this heat can't be good for my fragile teenage complexion."

"On the contrary," Joey chimed in, "it's called East Coast humidity. And it's quite good for the skin."

Pacey flicked Joey's ponytail teasingly. "But obviously not for the hair, Potter. Maybe you should consider a perm."

Joey smirked back. "What's with all the angst? Is

Brother Dougie making you sweat it up to the oldies again?"

"Richard Simmons is the least of my problems," said an exasperated Pacey. "Between papier-mâché-ing, yoga, and the *Cats* soundtrack, I can barely get a heterosexual thought in—"

Annoyed with the interruption to his evening entertainment, Dawson shot Pacey a look and indicated the TV.

Pacey continued, undeterred. "I refuse to believe Dougie and I are from the same gene pool."

Joey held out her hands to Pacey, palms up, "Save your whining for someone who cares."

Pacey shrugged at Joey's hands. "What?"

"Dishpan hands," Joey answered.

"Cry me a river, Potter," Pacey said as he rolled his eyes.

Joey sat up. "You try being trapped between a crying toddler and an endless stream of guests. I eat, sleep, and breathe the Potter B&B. And for what? Bed and Breakfast? It's more like Bored and Broke."

Dawson grabbed the remote and turned up the volume. Really loud.

Joey, finally noticing Dawson's annoyance, stopped her rant.

Pacey turned to watch the movie. "So, what's on the tube tonight?"

His eyes never veering from the TV, Dawson stated flatly, "*Summer School.* The phrase I wish you were having an intimate relationship with this vacation."

Pacey kicked off his shoes, exclaiming loudly, "No can do, Dawson. There will be no summer schooling for me. Pacey Witter is all yours!"

"Sounds kinky. Can I join in the fun?" A sultry voice teased. All heads turned to see Jen, her hair a lighter shade of blond, climbing through Dawson's window. As she positioned herself on the sill, Pacey noticed Jen's pale pink tank top. He smiled at the prominent bathing suit lines peeking out from underneath. Yes, while Joey was reaching for a dishtowel and cooking oil, all Jen had done for the past week was reach for a beach towel and tanning oil.

A woman after my own heart, Pacey thought to himself.

"Hasn't anyone ever heard of knocking?" Dawson snapped. "I'm trying to watch a movie here." Joey and Pacey shared a smile with newcomer Jen. The threesome had a perverse fondness for irritating their good friend.

Jen dangled her legs from the window. "I did knock, Dawson, but there was no answer. So, I decided to get a little crazy and pull a Joey." Indicating the TV, she smiled, "What's showing at the Leery Theater this evening?"

Dawson sighed, giving up. "For the third and final time, I'm trying to enjoy *Summer School.* A classic yet comedic tale of teen summer angst—"

Pacey laughed in amusement, "What do you need the TV for? Just watch us!"

Dawson rolled his eyes. "Sorry, but in entertainment quality, you guys get . . ." He mulled it over for a moment, then . . . "two thumbs down."

"Don't be so quick to charge eight bucks for a glimpse of your life either, Dawson," Joey retaliated. Jen and Pacey laughed in agreement.

Dawson looked around at his amused friends. "Very funny. But whose room did all of you choose to gather in tonight?" he asked smugly. Joey, Jen, and Pacey exchanged glances. Good point. Although they hated to admit it, they knew Dawson was at the core of their foursome. Aware of their discomfort, Dawson turned off the TV. "Okay, even I can admit that movie night is getting a little old. . . ."

Jen lunged backward out the window, pretending to throw herself out. "I'm sorry," she said, feigning shock, "did I just hear what I thought I heard?"

Joey egged her on. "I can see the front page of the *Capeside Herald* now. . . ." She did her best imitation. "Read all about it! Dawson Leery in a fit of heat exhaustion and cabin fever cancels movie night—forever!"

Dawson faked a smile. "Careful, or I'll start locking my window," he threatened. Joey and Jen exchanged glances. *Yeah, right.* Dawson shrugged. "Anyway, I have better plans for this summer than watching movies."

Jen mocked, "Let me guess. Making movies?"

Dawson shook his head, "Nope."

Nothing to do with movies? Joey was skeptical. This wasn't the Dawson she knew and once loved . . . or maybe still loved.

Dawson stood up and exclaimed, "Think about it. With college looming on the not-too-distant horizon, I'm going to do what any self-respecting teenager would do—"

"Get some nooky?" offered Pacey.

Dawson shook his head at Pacey's one-track mind and said, "No. Get an internship." The room went silent. Joey, Jen, and Pacey looked around at each other, curious.

Pacey put his hand on Dawson's forehead to see if he was feverish. "Work for free? Leery, are you mad?"

Jen piped in, questioning, "And just where do you plan to work for free in Boring-town, U.S.A.?"

Dawson frowned, answering, "I don't know exactly. But I want it to be somewhere adventurous, mindless, and fun."

Joey smiled. Adventurous—mindless—fun! That kind of internship sounded great. She asked Dawson curiously, "Have any ideas where you'll work?"

"I was thinking something outdoors, maybe by the sea," Dawson answered.

Joey smiled, recalling Dawson's recent movie rental, *Summer of '42.* "So the internship is just a vehicle for you to find an older woman who will tenderly guide you into manhood?"

Pacey stood up and asked excitedly, "Where do I sign up?"

Jen laughed. "That kind of experience happens once in a lifetime, Pacey. And I'm afraid your dance card has already been filled." Joey, Jen, and Dawson shared a laugh.

Pacey sat down on the bed, depressed. Jen was right. Losing his virginity to his beautiful C.H.S. English teacher was his once-in-a-lifetime, never-gonna-happen-again sexual jackpot.

Dawson smiled at Pacey. "Ah, but they can't take away the memories," he consoled. Pacey nodded in agreement. Dawson always had a way of cheering him up. Dawson glanced around at his friends. "So, you think you guys might want to join me?"

"With you, an older woman, and *Summer of 42*?" Joey snorted. "I think I'll pass."

"No!" said Dawson. "Do you guys want to do an internship with me?"

Jen groaned, "If you're suggesting that I work for free, let me just say . . . I don't think so!"

Pacey, quickly reconsidering his time with his brother, Deputy Doug, arose from the bed to leave. "You know, once you figure out the basics, papier-mâché can be incredibly relaxing." He headed for the door.

Dawson darted across the room and shut it before Pacey could exit. "Just hear me out . . . ten seconds is all I ask." Dawson took a deep breath. He looked inspired, driven almost. "Capeside must have something to offer the résumé-building teenage townie looking for an internship. And with said summer experience, said townie can gain acceptance to his or her preferred college and sail away from their said sorry seaside holiday they call home."

Joey listened, interested. Any escape from the Potter B&B, no matter how temporary, was sounding pretty good to her, especially if it could help her get into a good college. But then, she wasn't so sure about leaving her sister, Bessie, holding down the fort. But then, Bessie had just finished encouraging her to think about her future beyond the B&B. But then . . . Enough! Joey was driving herself crazy, with this flip-flopping. Adventurous—mindless—fun! That's what she wanted and that's what she needed. "I'll do it," Joey said matter-of-factly. "Where do I sign up?"

But as for Jen and Pacey, Dawson lost them at the word "internship." They each headed toward the window. As they climbed down to leave, Dawson thought fast. He yelled out the window after them, "And with Joey and I bettering ourselves as human beings, you two will be stuck having to entertain each other. And this time, my room is completely off-limits to whatever sick, utterly mindless sexual bargain you two conjure up."

Jen reached the lawn first. She looked up at Pacey making his way down the ladder and rolled her eyes at having been reminded of their short-lived, lip-locking days. Jen, about to cave in, looked up at Dawson. She groaned, "Well . . ."

Pacey, halfway down the ladder, jumped off and ran over, grabbing Jen. "Don't give in," he pleaded. "You'll be giving up two entire months of daytime TV! Think Oprah, think Rosie . . ."

Dawson counteroffered out the window, "Think of Grams's Bible group every afternoon at four."

Jen relented. "Okay," she yelled up to Dawson, "I'm in."

Pacey writhed in disbelief. "Lindley," he said, "you were my only hope."

Dawson smiled down at his friends. "So, we're all in agreement? If I find something cool, everyone will do it?"

Pacey begrudgingly nodded his head "yes." "Just promise me it won't start before ten o'clock in the morning," he demanded, "I need my beauty sleep."

Dawson sighed. His friends could be hard to please. "Anything else?" he asked.

Jen looked at Pacey and his raging hormones standing beside her. She piped in quickly, "Nothing involving Waldeck Island."

Pacey mocked, "C'mon, Jen. Don't you want another field trip filled with haunted woods, angry witches—"

"And a teenage love spell gone awry?" Jen disputed. "Absolutely not. No way. Not on your life." Jen looked up at Dawson with an icy stare. She meant it.

"Okay, okay. No Waldeck Island," Dawson promised.

"Party pooper," Pacey grumbled as he headed toward his home.

Jen shook her head at Pacey, then glanced up at Dawson. "Don't be hurt by his lack of interest. Pacey's attention deficit disorder prevents him from doing anything that requires his concentration for more than thirty seconds," she explained.

Pacey turned around and winked at Jen. "Anything nonsexual, that is," he bragged.

"And then you woke up," Jen laughed in disbelief.

As the twosome bickered toward their respective homes, Dawson watched them from his window. "Those two trade witty insults like baseball cards," he laughed to Joey.

"Yeah," Joey said softly. Slipping her sandals on to leave, she thought about her summer in Capeside two years ago. When it had just been the three of them—Dawson, Joey, and Pacey. The three of them against the world. Then Jen Lindley moved next door to Dawson and overactive hormones suddenly preempted their childhood games. That was the day when everything changed, when suddenly there were four instead of three, when growing up happened whether they resisted it or not. That was the day when Joey climbing in and out of Dawson's window took on a whole new meaning. And sometimes, though she would never admit it to anyone else but herself, Joey still resented Jen Lindley for moving to Capeside and cheating her out of her playmates. "Gotta go," Joey said, as she walked up behind Dawson.

Dawson turned around, disappointed. "You just got here," he complained. Joey shrugged. She was ready to leave just the same. "Oh, come on," Dawson begged, "I'll put in another summer classic. This one's a classic that I know you'll enjoy."

"I'll take a rain check," Joey said. She headed out the window. "See you tomorrow, Dawson."

Dawson watched her go. "See ya, Joe," he whispered back, softly, disappointed that she hadn't stayed.

Later that night Dawson was lying on his bed, the wind blowing slightly, the curtains billowing out. His eyes were glued to the TV but he wasn't watching *Jaws* or *E.T.* or any other of Spielberg's classics. He was watching his own movie, his first movie, *Sea Creatures from the Deep*. On the screen was Joey, beautiful Joey, sunning herself on the dock, completely unsuspecting and oblivious to the hideous creature emerging behind her. Pacey, disguised as the Sea Creature, grabbed her and her beach chair, yanking her into the creek. Dawson laughed, watching the movie. He remembered how many takes it took to get that shot right. He remembered how Joey had complained that Pacey was trying to cop a feel. He remembered how somewhere deep down, although he hadn't come to terms with it yet, he knew that this was the girl he loved.

A noise outside drew Dawson's attention away from the TV. He stared at the window for a few moments, his mind playing games. Finally, as he gathered his courage to go check it out, Joey's head popped into the window frame. "And while you're at it," she said, smiling, "no haunted houses, castles, or mansions, either."

"What?" Dawson questioned, his nerves rattled.

Joey climbed into the room. "I got home and started thinking," she explained. "I know you promised Jen that there would be no Waldeck Island. But I don't want our internship to be any-place that's creepy, scary, or remotely spooky."

"Done," Dawson agreed, as he made room for Joey on his bed.

Joey plopped down beside him. "You promise?" she asked tentatively.

Glad that Joey had come back to join him for the movie, Dawson assured her, "I absolutely promise." Dawson didn't want to do anything creepy, scary, or remotely spooky. Waldeck Island wasn't exactly a walk in the park for Dawson either. He didn't need to see the sequel to that *Blair Witch Project* in the making. He just wanted a fun, relaxing, memorable summer with his best friends. He wanted to relive the fun and excitement of past summers.

Joey noticed the TV and smiled. "This is defi-nitely a classic." She and Dawson settled in to watch their movie.

2

Woodland Beach

The Leery SUV pulled into Woodland Beach's small gravel parking lot. Situated atop a mountainous cliff, the area overlooked a sloping, sandy beach and the rolling Atlantic Ocean. To the north, on a jagged bluff, a weathered lighthouse towered above the crashing waves. To the south, a lone research vessel docked at the jetty. And directly below, banking the shoreline, was a wildlife aquarium surrounded by murky tidal pools.

Dawson and Joey, dragging a sleepy-eyed Jen and an even sleepier Pacey, climbed out of the parked vehicle. The waves were so loud Pacey had to whine a notch louder to be heard. "I thought we agreed: nothing before ten o'clock."

Dawson slammed his car door shut, irritated. "This was the only time we could interview, Pacey. Sorry if it impedes on your eight hours."

Jen yawned. "Where are we again?" she asked drowsily. "Was this the one where we help children through art?"

Joey noticed an old gray clapboard building tucked neatly in the surrounding birch forest. She pointed to the camouflaged structure that stood a few yards away. "We're at the Oceanographic Institute."

"The Oceano-what?" Pacey questioned.

Dawson threw his hands up, exasperated. "Woodland Beach, Pacey. I could have sworn you were in my room when I found it online."

Pacey shrugged. "I didn't notice."

Dawson frowned. "What did you think I was doing on my desktop all that time?" he questioned.

"Same thing I do," Pacey laughed. "Sitting in a chat room, telling gullible people you're a Brad Pitt look-alike with a big—"

Kicking sand on him, Joey cut him off quickly. "Shut up, Pacey."

"I was going to say a big bank account. And don't be so quick to snap, Potter," Pacey retorted, looking down over the cliff. "It's a long way down."

Joey marched off toward the building. "I'm officially making another request, Dawson. My internship cannot involve working with any large dumb animals . . . specifically, Pacey."

Pacey followed Joey, feigning hurt. "Is that any

way to treat a friend?" Joey tried to suppress a smile. Pacey's outgoing personality opened him up to ridicule.

Dawson followed behind his friends. "If this is what the entire summer is going to consist of, I should just do this alone," he muttered.

Jen, sluggish, stumbled behind. "Good idea. And in that case, I'll be waiting in the car."

As Jen turned to leave, Pacey grabbed her jacket. "Oh no, Lindley," he exclaimed, "I stay, you stay."

Reaching the building, Dawson opened the front door. "Well, I, for one, am out of here," he hollered. He marched into the Institute, the door slamming behind him.

Dawson was in the process of filling out his application, when Joey, Pacey, and Jen finally found their way down the long, empty hallway and joined him. Dawson walked over, grabbed a few more applications off the counter, and handed them to his accepting friends. And that was that. All was forgiven.

Joey took her application and sat beside Dawson on a wooden bench lining the wall. Pacey took a seat on the bench opposite them and made room for Jen, who sat down, defeated. Unless she stole the keys to the Mitchmobile from Dawson, she wasn't going anywhere. Dawson stared at his application, puzzled. He read aloud to himself, "Hobbies?"

Joey looked at him, oddly. "Hello? Try film making."

Dawson laughed. "Film making is hardly a hobby, Joe. It's my life."

Joey gave Dawson a classic Joey Potter look. "Just write it down."

Pacey looked at his paper, frowning, pen in his mouth. "I'm stuck, too," he complained.

"Witter has two t's," Jen quipped. That got a laugh out of Joey and a look of death from Pacey.

Jen smiled, apologetic. "Seriously. What's the trouble, Pacey?" she asked.

"References," he answered.

"As in . . . ?" Jen looked at him blankly.

"I have none," Pacey complained.

"What about a favorite teacher," offered Jen.

"Right," Pacey joked. "I can see the phone call now . . ." Imitating his old teacher, "Yes, this is Mr. Peterson. . . . Sure, I know Pacey Witter. . . . He is a very precise and exact young man. . . . Take, for instance, the time he spat on me. He aimed for my left eye and was right on target." Jen nodded her head in agreement. Pacey didn't always lend himself to good impressions. He came from the act-first-think-later mentality, the complete opposite of Dawson.

Dawson glanced at Joey. Not too long ago, he had tried to win her affection by being more like Pacey. But it hadn't worked. And he had known it wouldn't. For in his heart, Dawson knew the only way to secure a romance with Joey was to remain steady and true.

Joey noticed Dawson's far-off look and broke the

silence. She blurted out teasingly, "How about Ms. Jacobs, Pacey. I'm sure she left you a forwarding hotel room." Jen and Dawson laughed, remembering Pacey's sophomore-year drama.

"Pipe down, Potter," Pacey muttered. "Those English teacher 'Pinter moments' are precious to my heart."

"What about Buzz's mom?" Dawson asked. Pacey had been a great mentor to young Buzz, even if he did let him eat an unlimited amount of sugar and hot dogs.

"Good call, Dawson," Pacey said, writing it down. He smiled, happy that he did have a reference, after all. He gave Joey a satisfied smirk, but before Joey could engage in any more Potter–Witter banter, a young, attractive woman appeared. "Hi, guys," she said, looking down at her paperwork. "You must be Dawson, Joey, Jen, and Pacey. I'm Kate Fields, the Office Manager and Internship Coordinator here at Woodland Beach."

Pacey looked her up and down. "Why, yes. Yes, you are," he mumbled happily to himself. Pacey was in high hopes that his "dance card" would be put back in use. Dawson, Joey, and Jen shot Pacey disapproving looks.

"I'd like to meet with each of you individually to go over your qualifications and your interests," Kate said, as she ran her fingers through her long, thick, red hair, "So, who's first?"

Pacey jumped forward. "I'll go. I'm really eager to get started."

Dawson, Jen, and Joey exchanged glances. Pacey's change of heart was obviously inspired by a short skirt, a great smile, and two very long legs.

As they walked toward her office, Kate scanned Pacey's application. "This is very impressive, Pacey. . . ." She continued reading. "Wow . . . you volunteered for the Wildlife Rescue Reserve."

Pacey shrugged, modestly. "I have a strong love for animals as well as my community," he explained.

Joey shook her head at Dawson and Jen. "Watching Deputy Dougie save a cat in a tree doesn't qualify as Wildlife Rescue," she remarked.

Kate entered her office, with Pacey at her heels. Pacey poked his head out the door. "Don't wait up, kids. We might be a while."

While Pacey was interviewing with Kate, Jen kept from falling asleep by champing on a wad of pink bubble gum. "This doesn't seem so bad," Jen said, looking at a pamphlet. "I thought I'd be locked away in a small, dank office—filing papers, answering phones, making coffee, typing memos, constantly pulling up a constricting pair of panty hose. . . ."

Meanwhile, Joey and Dawson passed the time thumb wrestling. Joey threw up her hands, aggravated. "You cheated."

Dawson was adamant. "I did not."

"Yes, you did. You're hiding your thumb behind your knuckles and waiting to attack."

Dawson shrugged his shoulders, not seeing the problem. "So?"

"So? That's cheating. Number one rule of the game. No hiding of the thumb. This is thumb wrestling, not guerrilla warfare."

Dawson laughed, giving in. "Okay, best two out of three."

"Fine," Joey sighed.

Jen continued to flip through the pamphlet, happily. "Sitting out on a beach, with the sun, sea, sky and sand, and a good looking graduate student . . ." Yep, Woodland Beach was beginning to look pretty good to Jen Lindley.

Finally, after what seemed to be an eternity, Pacey emerged from Kate's office all smiles. "I'm happy to report Woodland Beach has a place for all of us," he bragged.

Joey looked at her watch with a frown. "And how do you figure that, Pacey? In the last hour and a half, Ms. Field's only interviewed you."

Kate walked out of her office. "Please, call me Kate. And I apologize for keeping all of you waiting. Pacey was just so interesting. You know, I used to date his older brother, Doug, in high school." She sighed. "Until he dumped me at the prom."

Mesmerized by Kate's intense blue eyes, Pacey turned to his friends and explained, "After Kate complimented me on my Witter good looks and I comforted her with Dougie's closeted homosexuality, I gave her a quick rundown of our unique talents."

"Is that so . . . ?" Joey inquired, suspicious of his motives.

"Yes," Kate answered. "And you four are an impressive group of young achievers . . . mentoring troubled children, fund-raising for the Capeside Orphanage, an anti-prom party to prevent student discrimination."

Jen popped a bubble, ready to hit the beach. "Just slap us with our summer slave duties, Kate. We can take it."

Kate, walking down the hall, gestured for the group to follow, "Okay, then. C'mon. I'll give you guys a tour of the Institute and tell you what your Internships will entail." Without missing a beat, Pacey rushed off to catch up with her.

He clapped his hands and rubbed them together, whispering in Dawson's ear as he ran by, "Tamara Jacobs: The Sequel."

Dawson shook his head and stood up to follow Kate and Pacey. Throwing his application into the trash, he smiled at Joey and Jen. Despite Pacey's smugness, he had gotten them out of a tedious interview. "Works for me," he said, pleased.

At the end of the hall, Kate guided the group into a large, two-story room. "This is the Taylor Museum," she informed. Joey, Jen, and Pacey scanned the large collection of photographs, sea charts, prints, and journals. Dawson was particularly fascinated with a very large optical machine.

"What is that?" Dawson asked.

Kate walked over to the device. "It's an underwater camera."

"Awesome," Dawson said, very impressed.

Kate smiled, "From what Pacey told me about your interest in film making, I thought you'd like it." He did. Dawson checked out the camera. He was intrigued. Kate continued, "And who knows, with your film experience the Institute might just grant you a test dive with it." Dawson smiled at the thought of himself on, or under, the high seas.

Jen walked over and teased, "That's probably not the best idea. Our little buddy hasn't had much luck with boats."

"Really? Like what?" Kate questioned Dawson, concerned.

Jen, answering for Dawson, exclaimed, "Take your pick. There was the time when his raging hormones drove him and his blond bombshell seductress onto a dock. It cost this lover boy two thousand dollars and guaranteed his continued virginity—" Dawson frowned. This was getting just a little too personal.

Joining in their conversation, Pacey added, "Or how about the time when his Joey jealousies almost killed me and two hundred spectators when he refused to yield to a regatta right-of-way!"

"Okay," Dawson exclaimed. He turned to Kate, confident, "I have excellent boating abilities and would be happy to provide you with any needed references."

Kate quickly dismissed the concern. "Don't

worry, **Dawson**. You'll be spending your internship on shore, assisting a BU graduate participating in our Summer Studies Program."

"Doing what?" Dawson questioned.

"Investigating facts in the museum's Rare Books Room," Kate answered. A summer locked away in a library? Dawson's disappointment was obvious, but Kate was sympathetic. "I know it's not a summer in the sun, but, as consolation, you can put together a short documentary of the project's research methods and findings." That sounded a little better to Dawson.

He probed further. "So what is this project that I'll be filming?"

"An independent search for a whaling vessel that went down off the coast in 1852," Kate explained.

"So, there is a chance of an off-shore salvage?" Dawson asked. This could be a great opportunity for him.

Kate wasn't optimistic. "Grad students have been looking for the Breckinridge vessel for over seventy years. So far, no one's found anything but a dead-end." Dawson took a last look at the underwater camera, wondering what his chances were of finding the wreckage. Dawson had hit a lot of dead-ends in the last few years—it was time for a road that actually led somewhere.

Meanwhile, Joey and Pacey had ventured upstairs into what soon would be Dawson's home away from home, The Taylor Museum's Rare Books

Room. It looked more like an old musty parlor than a library. Wooden tables, antique chairs and a dusty, dark wood floor. Pacey ventured farther into the room. He came upon a small door with an old crystal doorknob. . . .

"C'mon, Pacey. Hurry up. We probably shouldn't be up here," Joey hollered nervously as she strained her neck to see where Pacey had roamed. Eager to go back downstairs, Joey had stayed near the staircase. With no response from Pacey, she leaned against the wall and waited. Feeling a chill behind her, she turned around abruptly. But nothing was there except for the old faded Currier and Ives wallpaper pasted to the wall. Intrigued by the design, Joey took a closer look. The panoramic seascape pictures hidden within the homespun colors were mesmerizing.

While she was examining the wallpaper, Pacey turned the crystal doorknob and looked into the closet. But nothing was inside. Oddly, the space was so small, it could hardly house a broom. Pacey shrugged his shoulders, "What's the point?" he pondered, closing the door.

Fascinated, Joey rubbed the rich, historical wallpaper. As she brushed her fingers against the dry paper, it crackled. But Joey thought she heard something else. A child's voice? Curious, she placed her ear close to the wall. A little girl's faint moan cried out from within the print. "Play with me, Josephine," she urged. Joey jumped back, startled.

"Let's go!" Pacey interrupted. "There's nothing up here but a bunch of boring old books." Shaken, Joey turned around nervously. Pacey looked at her ashen skin. "You look like you've just seen a ghost," he said, hopping down the stairs. Worried her imagination was getting the best of her, Joey quickly followed him.

In the now empty Rare Books Room, the crystal doorknob of the small closet door shuddered and rotated slightly, tentatively. The wood around the doorknob creaked gently. "Play with me, Josephine. . . . Play with me . . . ," a whispering voice cried.

Back outside, Kate guided the group down a steep cobblestone path toward the oceanfront. "Woodland Beach is an unpolluted, deep-water port with an abundance of marine and wild life," she asserted. "Just look around you. There are colorful seashells, Monarch butterflies, and—"

"Ow!" Jen yelled, jumping back and accidentally pushing Joey into the sand. The group turned to see a snapping turtle bury itself under a grassy dune. Jen glared at it, shocked. "That sucker nipped me for spite."

"No, it just thought your big toe was dinner," Joey quipped, standing up. Dusting the sand off herself, she explained, "Your flowery sandals and flirty red nail polish make your feet look like a family of sand crabs." Dawson and Pacey tried hard to control their laughter.

"Everyone, just shut up," Jen yelled.

Kate looked at the bickering foursome. "How long have you guys been friends?" she asked.

Jen snipped, sarcastically, "Oh, did you get the idea we were actually friends?"

"I hope this contentiousness won't be a problem," Kate said to Jen. "You and Pacey will be sharing your summer internship duties at the aquarium," she divulged.

"A summer with Lindley looking at my Speedos!" Pacey winked at Jen, teasing.

"Oh, no!" Jen exclaimed. "The only things allowed to surface in those aquarium waters are the fish."

Kate agreed. "Standard bathing suits, rubber boots, sunscreen and insect repellent is the required uniform," she pronounced as she gestured to the group to continue down the hill. The group followed silently—Jen favoring her foot, Pacey fascinated with Kate, his redheaded Oceano-Goddess, Dawson pondering a possible sea salvage, and Joey, wondering about the whispering wallpaper and questioning her sanity.

At the bottom of the hill was a large marshy area with a huge wire-screened building situated in its midst. "Is that it?" Jen asked, disillusioned.

Pacey teased, "What were you expecting, Jen, Sea World?"

Jen replied, "Well, I was hoping for something a little more cheerful than *Children of the Corn's Creekside Vacation!*"

Pacey wrapped his arms around Jen. "Don't worry, Lindley. I'll protect you from the big bad fishies."

Using a heavy silver key clasped to a chain around her neck, Kate unlocked a large screen door. "Let's go inside," she said. "I think you'll be pleasantly surprised."

The aquarium was a mystical, mysterious sea-life kingdom, and its atmosphere was something reminiscent of an overgrown English garden. Trees, moss, and sand surrounded various shaped tidal pools. Carved rock stands held up large glass tanks. "We have twelve tanks filled with regional fish and shellfish. And there are a total of three hands-on pools where we keep the larger marine animals," Kate boasted.

Pacey wasn't all that impressed. "I was hoping for something a little more like *Baywatch,*" he admitted. "Lindley would look great in one of those sexy red bathing suits."

Jen ignored the sexual harassment by her now co-worker and walked over to the largest pool. She dipped her aching toe into the water. Suddenly, a seven-foot dolphin jumped into the air. She jumped back in surprise. "Whoa," Jen yelled.

Dawson, Joey, and Pacey rushed over, curious. "Holy Moby Dick!" Pacey shouted.

Kate walked over and threw the playful big gray bottlenose a fish. "Meet Abigail, the newest addition at Woodland Beach. She was found floating offshore two weeks ago, dehydrated and malnourished. Probably got caught in a fishing net. . . ."

"What did you say her name was?" Jen interrupted.

"Abigail," Kate responded. Pacey, Dawson, and Joey shifted uneasily.

Jen frowned. "Her last name wouldn't be Morgan, would it?" she asked.

Kate reasoned, "We haven't given her a last name. But, if you'd like—"

Jen glanced down at Abigail. "No, that's okay," she muttered quickly. Jen studied the dolphin, looking for any similarities to her former friend and, at times, enemy, Abby Morgan. Halfway through tenth grade, after Dawson dumped Jen for Joey, Jen had felt left out in the cold. It was Abby Morgan who had reached out to her then. Abby Morgan had a classic way of saying exactly what other people felt, but were too polite to say. She was a true individual . . . not always a nice, or kind, or thoughtful individual, but an individual nonetheless. Abby Morgan taught Jen one of the hardest life lessons she'd ever learned. On a cold night, after too much champagne, Jen watched Abby call her a "bitch" and then accidentally fall off a dock to her death. Never again would Jen discount life's powerful karma.

Kate continued on, "Most of your time will be spent feeding the mammals and cleaning their tanks. In the mornings you and Pacey will gather and inventory shellfish off the beach. And in the afternoons, you'll exercise Abigail."

Pacey walked over to the side of the pool and gestured the dolphin over to him. Abigail happily swam over and started doing tricks. Pacey was amazed. Jen smiled at the friendly dolphin and walked over. While it wasn't *Baywatch*, neither she nor Pacey could resist this loving, playful, and rather large pet.

"Does she always smile so much?" Jen asked Kate, intrigued.

"Yep. Bottlenose dolphins have a constant grin on their faces, Jen. The shape of their 'beaks' gives them a permanent smile."

As Kate continued to tell Jen and Pacey about their summer duties, Joey and Dawson walked around the aquarium, in awe.

"This place is beautiful," Joey exclaimed.

Dawson stopped to gaze into one of the smaller tidal pools. It was stuffed with large, fat orange goldfish. "Yeah," Dawson said, his mind a million miles away. He reached into his pocket and pulled out a penny.

"Don't throw that into the pools," said Kate. "Pennies can harm the fish."

Chastened, Dawson slipped the coin back into his pocket, but not before wishing that he and Joey would find their way back to each other. Opening his eyes, he handed another coin to Joey. "Make a wish anyway," he encouraged. Joey accepted the coin, appreciative, but skeptical. Even in a spiritual environment such as this, she still wasn't ready to believe in pennies that made wishes come true.

"Come on, Joe," Dawson persisted. "Just one little wish. No harm, no foul . . . No chance, no gain . . . No—"

"Okay, okay," Joey said, taking the coin from Dawson. She concentrated on the coin. Then she threw it across the room and bopped an unsuspecting Pacey in the head.

"Ow!" Pacey yelled. He looked around, wondering what just happened. Dawson and Joey giggled. They walked over to rejoin their friends.

"What did you wish for?" Dawson asked Joey.

"A helmet," Pacey joked. "Because you'll wish you had one when I hurl this penny at your head, Potter." Joey laughed.

"I'm sorry, Pacey." She shrugged her shoulders. "Bad aim, what can I say?"

Dawson persisted. "Joey," he asked again, "What was your wish?"

"If I tell you, then my wish won't come true," she teased.

"C'mon, I'll tell you what I wished for," he bribed.

"I don't want to know, Dawson," Joey said.

Dawson frowned, giving up his inquisition. "Fine. I don't really care anyway," he lied. He was desperate to know if his name was any part of Joey's wish. But it hadn't been.

Joey had wished for mindless fun. She wanted to revert back to the days when all she worried about was keeping her shoes tied and her hair unknotted. When there were no decisions harder than choos-

ing beets, applesauce, or cottage cheese as her side dish for dinner. A time when she could go to sleep and fly in her dreams, not drown.

Dawson and Joey stepped up to the side of the pool beside Jen and Pacey. Abigail was jumping through a Hula-Hoop for Pacey as Jen dangled her feet in the pool, amused at their show. Things seemed to be looking up. Well, until Abigail splashed a huge wave of water right over Jen. Pacey doubled over with laughter. Jen was definitely not amused. She took one look at Pacey and knew what she had to do. She shoved him into the pool.

Everyone laughed. Instinctively helpful to humans, Abigail tried to rescue this poor boy in need. She swam over to Pacey and nudged him to the side of the pool. Freaked, Pacey quickly began splashing the water to get to the side. Thinking he was flailing, Abigail surged under the water and lifted him in between his legs, flipping him onto her back. Keeping him afloat, she swam over and deposited Pacey on the side of the pool. Pacey frowned. "I'd hoped to see a little action this summer, but not with a fish."

"Don't worry, Pace, Abigail's standards are probably too high to even consider you," Jen teased. Jen, Joey, and Dawson shared a laugh. Kate usually disapproved of such antics but she couldn't help but laugh, too.

"Abigail's not a fish, Pacey. She's a cetacean. Cetaceans have the shape of fish and live in water, but they are really mammals. Just like whales and porpoises."

"What's the difference?" Jen asked.

"Fish are cold-blooded, breathe through gills, and are hatched from eggs. Mammals are animals that are born alive and feed on their mothers' milk. They breathe air and are warm-blooded," Kate advised.

Pacey looked down at Abigail peering up at him from the side of the pool. "Warm-blooded and frisky," he smiled.

Kate offered a hand to help Pacey stand. "Which is why we need to always be careful and follow the rules of the aquarium." She glanced at Jen, continuing, "And that includes no foul play around the pool."

Jen nodded. "No more pushing Pacey in, I promise."

Back at the parking lot where they had started, Joey was getting impatient. "So what will my internship be?" she questioned Kate.

Kate pointed to the north. "Joey, you'll be spending your time up there."

Joey looked over to see the stone lighthouse perched high on the cliff. Even on a sunny day, Joey suspected it would look scary and intimidating. "Way up there?" she questioned.

"Sure," Kate answered. "Manor Light has a most spectacular view of Cape Cod. We open it to the public for the summer. You'll be giving tours."

Joey glanced up at the lighthouse again. She really didn't like the looks of it. "Um . . .well . . ."

"Joey, you'll love it. Manor Light has a fascinating history. Built in the year 1840, this lighthouse has helped many a ship out at sea. We retired her in 1956, and, yet, she's still standing—enduring the elements."

"Well . . ." Joey said, studying the lighthouse.

Kate continued to persuade, "And again, the view from the Manor Light is spectacular. From forty-two feet high, you'll see how incredible the ocean looks. On sunny days it casts a metallic sparkle of silvers, coppers, and golds."

Dawson placed his arm on Joey's shoulder, excited for her. "Just think, Joe. On your break you could paint from up there." Joey smiled at the thought of jumping back into her art. It had been a while since she had worked on a project. But still, something nagged her about the lighthouse.

Joey looked around at the group. Dawson, Pacey, and Jen had each accepted their assignments. She couldn't allow herself to be the only quitter. "Well, if the lighthouse is where you see me, then that's what I would like to do," Joey smiled, lying.

Kate was impressed. "Now that's the kind of attitude I'm looking for around here." Kate extended her hand to the foursome, "Welcome to Woodland Beach." Their summer had begun.

The ride back to Capeside was a quiet one. Each of the four were lost in their own expectations as to what the summer held in store.

Seated in the backseat of the car, Pacey day-dreamed as he watched the rural landscape speed by his window. If anyone was closest to the mindset of Joey, it was him. In the last two years, Pacey had been in love three times. This summer, he didn't want to find love. His heart was still digesting his memories of the past. Nope, Pacey wanted to have fun. He wanted to have fun with a cute redhead named Kate.

"Kate's a hottie, don't you think?" he asked Dawson, tapping him on the back.

Dawson glanced in his rearview mirror and smiled at his friend. "Yes, she sure is," he agreed, looking back at the road. A bird dropping plopped onto the windshield. Dawson flicked his wind-shield wiper to whisk it away. It smeared across the glass. Dawson frowned. He had a feeling he would be washing his car a lot this summer.

"What kind of a guy do you think Kate goes for?" Pacey asked, continuing to encourage the conver-sation.

"Hoping it will be the Witter kind?" Dawson asked, already knowing the answer.

"More like dreaming," Pacey said, fishing for a compliment. "She's the most beautiful woman I've ever seen." But all this statement received was dis-believing stares from Joey and Jen.

"More beautiful than me?" Jen questioned.

"Definitely," Pacey stated, without missing a beat.

Joey turned around to look at Pacey, intrigued.

"Do tell, Pacey. On a scale from one to ten—where do Kate, Jen, and myself fall on your attractive continuum?"

Pacey knew better than to go down this road, so he went for rude instead. "Kate is the beauty scale on which you two hopefuls slide back and forth, depending on the amount of work you invest on yourselves in the morning." he answered. Dawson laughed. Joey reached back and jabbed Pacey. Jen turned her head toward the window, ditching the conversation for her earlier, and more fulfilling, daydream.

Jen was reflecting on her bedroom. Grams was driving her crazy to do the spring cleaning Jen had put off until summer. Jen didn't want to change her environment. She was finally comfortable. She liked her room, her things, her mess, just the way they stood. She didn't see the need for a good organizing and dusting. "Out with the old, and in with the new," Grams would encourage. Jen had grown comfortable with Grams's needlepoint hangings, lace curtains, and patchwork quilt. She no longer craved miniblinds or a fashionable duvet.

Jen's mind trailed to Abigail. She wondered if the dolphin was happy at Woodland Beach. She felt sorry for it being separated from its herd. Jen knew how hard it was to leave a home and family and begin again in another. It wasn't easy, and it could be very lonely. Jen glanced at her three friends. While confident in her acceptance, sometimes Jen wished, if just for once, she could be the Manor Light—the old constant—in their group.

"So, Woodland Beach was a pretty good choice, huh?" Dawson asked, stirring up conversation.

"Yep, sure, mmn-hmn," Joey, Pacey, and Jen answered, caught up in their daydreams.

"Yep, Woodland Beach was a great choice," Dawson applauded himself as he drove them home to Capeside. And all of them were eager to begin work at Woodland Beach. All of them except . . .

3
Mary Breckinridge

It's just a lighthouse. It's just a lighthouse. It's just a lighthouse, Joey thought to herself. It was the following morning and she and the gang were headed toward Woodland Beach for their first official day as interns. While Dawson, Pacey, and Jen debated about why no one had invented a purse for men, Joey stared intently out the window. She couldn't figure out what was getting her so freaked out about Manor Light. Sure, she had been scared getting stranded on Waldeck Island. Thick forests, lost after dark, legends of ghostly witches . . . but here . . . here, she was safe. She was in Dawson's SUV heading to work at the Oceanographic Institute.

The other lighthouse tour guides probably hadn't complained, so she wouldn't either. But Joey couldn't get yesterday's episode in the Rare Books Room out of her head. Retelling the story to Bessie, she had felt woozy, but her sister was convinced that it was Joey's low blood sugar causing her slight dizzy spell. Bessie's remedy to the whispering wallpaper was an extra glass of orange juice at breakfast and an added chocolate bar in Joey's paper bag for lunch. "A lighthouse is a beacon for safety, a guide for lost ships," Joey told herself firmly. Manor Light had guided sailors through fogs, storms, and at times, probably their fears.

The SUV barreled down the last straightaway into Woodland Beach. Full of classic Leery optimism and enthusiasm, Dawson parked the car. Joey frowned at Manor Light looming on the cliff.

"What's with the long face, Joe?" Dawson questioned.

"Probably thinking about that haunted lighthouse," Pacey quipped.

"What?" Joey asked, snapping out of her trance.

"Don't tell me you haven't heard about the local legend, Potter," he teased. "Dougie used to threaten to lock me up in there if I didn't stop pulling the insides out of his George Michael cassettes."

"What legend?" Joey asked, suspicious. "I've lived here all my life. How come I haven't heard of any Lighthouse Legend?"

"You were too concerned with your very own

Leery legend living across the Creek," Pacey kidded.

"Funny," Joey answered, not amused. "And if this is a joke . . . ?" she threatened.

"Just tell us the legend," Jen said, intrigued.

"There's really not that much to tell," Pacey shrugged, his voice resonating otherwise. "Just that a spirit, a little girl's angry spirit, lives in the lighthouse."

Joey was mortified. "Are you telling me the lighthouse, the very lighthouse I will be working in every day, is supposedly haunted?"

"Apparently," Pacey smiled. "And I'm afraid it's not a very nice story," he added, shaking his head.

Pacey took a moment before pouring out the details. Everyone quieted. The surrounding trees flickered morning sunlight across the windows. As if setting the stage for the campfire tale, Pacey lowered his voice to a dramatic whisper. . . .

"Midnight, 1852," he said. "A small whaling vessel drew toward shore. An unexpected storm rolled in. The swelling waves were so large and fierce the sailors couldn't see a foot ahead of them. Sadly, Manor Light's beacon failed to signal them safely to shore. The ship bobbed in the water like a cork in a tub. Suddenly, a low horn was heard in the distance. The crew took a risk and steered a course toward the beckoning, unidentifiable sound—maybe a mermaid luring them to their death. The ship crashed against the jetty rocks. The hull sheared in two. The mast snapped like a tree branch. And the waves pulled the wreckage back out to sea, where it sank." Pacey notched up the drama. "All of the people aboard died, their lungs full of saltwater, their tortured eyes sinking into their black velvety graves. The only victim to wash ashore was an eight-year-old girl. Her body was buried by a small tree on the cliff. It is said that she haunts Manor Light to take revenge for her and her parents' dark, icy deaths."

The group sat silent. Finally, Dawson spoke. "It's just a legend, Joe," he comforted.

"So was Waldeck Island," Joey snapped. "And there we all were, running for our lives." Jen and Pacey glanced at Dawson in agreement. Waldeck Island had been an unsuspecting nightmare for all of them.

Joey stepped out of the car. "So much for promises," she said to Dawson, slamming the door. Grabbing her backpack, she slung it over one shoulder and headed down to the beach. "And so much for my 'beacon of safety,' " she added. "It's just a lighthouse," she reminded herself.

As Joey headed toward the lighthouse, Dawson, Jen, and Pacey made their way down the path toward the Institute. Dawson strained to keep Joey in his sight. Pacey was on the lookout for Kate. Jen busily divided her and Pacey's assigned aquarium duties.

"Okay, Pacey. You can take the tank facilities—" Jen offered.

"What's that?" Dawson asked.

"Squids, snails, and puppy dog tails," Pacey advised, frowning.

"All of Pacey's domain," Jen encouraged.

"Fine. If my place is with the salamanders, then you get to do the digging," Pacey bargained.

"What digging?" Dawson asked.

"At the seashore," Jen responded. "Seashells, seaweed, and anything else that smells particularly bad," she explained.

"And that includes having to take care of Abigail," Pacey further negotiated. It was a hard bargain. Jen liked the dolphin. But, in a weird way, the temperamental dolphin even looked like Abby.

"But I thought you two had something special starting up?" Jen teased.

Pacey refused. "No way, keep *Free Willy* away from this Witter. There's only room enough in my life for one sleek female companion."

Dawson frowned, "Willy's character in the movie was a whale, Pacey."

Pacey smiled. "And dolphins are a type of whale, Dawson. Someone wasn't paying attention to Kate's introductory speech yesterday! Cetaceans! Repeat after me . . . sih-TAY-shuns."

Jen lamented, tired of his pronunciations, "Okay, I'll take care of Abigail, but you do everything else. And that includes all of the daily feedings."

"Fine." Pacey agreed.

"Agreed," Jen confirmed. She added, "And I'd like a cheeseburger, medium Coke, and large fries," as she turned down the path toward the aquarium.

"Ring it up somewhere else," Pacey complained.

"Hello? Daily feedings! That includes me!" Jen smiled, victorious.

"Fine, I'll bring it over right after I clean your tank," Pacey smiled.

"In your dreams, Lunch Boy," Jen retorted.

"See what I have to put up with, Leery?" Pacey moaned to Dawson as he followed Jen toward the aquarium.

Dawson watched them walk away. Compared to the rest of them, he had it easy. While Joey was stressing about a haunted lighthouse and Jen and Pacey were arguing over cone snails, he would be playing Pirate. Yes, it seemed Dawson was the only one who had any hope of enjoying his internship. Hands shoved into the pockets of his khakis, Dawson walked into the Institute and headed toward the museum.

Inside the museum, Dawson ventured over to the staircase. A good-looking, twenty-something guy emerged overhead on the balcony. Dark hair, green eyes, and a sheer island shirt, he looked like a windblown sailor.

"Permission to come . . . up?" Dawson asked.

The guy looked down. "You must be my not-really-hired help," he joked.

Dawson walked up the stairs and extended his hand. "Free labor, otherwise known as Dawson

Leery," he greeted. The guy reached over and shook Dawson's hand.

"Nick Phelps. Permission granted," he boomed.

Dawson stepped into the Rare Books Room. "So," he asked curiously, "think we'll be spending our time in here, or venturing onto the high seas?"

"We'll see," Nick said. "Ever heard of the Breckinridges?" he questioned, pulling a book off the shelf.

Dawson thought for a moment. "Doesn't ring a bell." He took a seat on a leather sofa and propped his head on his hands. Ever the film maker, he was always up for a good story.

Nick told the tale. "In the 1800s, the Breckinridges, a young married couple from England, were bringing their only daughter, Mary, across the ocean to live in America. The ship was nearly to shore when a violent storm hit. Sadly, the sea was so fierce, the ship crashed on the rocks and the wreckage was swept back out to sea. Neither the parents nor the little girl survived. The ship has never been found."

Dawson's eyes widened. "Mary wouldn't be the same little girl that haunts Manor Light?" he questioned, intrigued.

"So, you have heard of the story." Nick smiled, pleased. But Dawson still wasn't sold. The Breckinridge drama had the makings of a good film, but something just wasn't sitting right.

"It's sounds more like a fictional legend," Dawson asserted.

Nick handed a book to Dawson. "I won't speak for the haunting at the lighthouse, but the Breckinridge shipwreck is no legend. It's a sad fact. And it's all right there in the Manor Light captain's log," he assured.

Dawson looked at the aged book in his hands, "What exactly do you plan to do?"

Nick smiled. "We're gonna raise the sunken ship!"

Dawson added, "But first we have to find it!"

Nick frowned at Dawson. "Just a minor detail," Nick said, confidently. "You see, in the last two summers I, myself, have become somewhat of a legend around these New England ports."

"Oh really?" Dawson asked, skeptical.

"Yep. The last two ships I searched for, I found." Nick leaned against the wall, daydreaming. "And who knows, maybe on this expedition, I'll find Mary Breckinridge's ghost, too!"

Meanwhile, Joey was thinking about anything but ghosts as she walked out on the cliff toward the lighthouse. The sea below her sounded loud and beautiful. As she listened to the rhythm of the waves, she took in the amazing view. An energetic seagull fishing in the surf made her laugh. Far out toward the horizon, the sky was as blue as she had ever seen. Joey smiled, a bit calmer. Cape Cod really was a peaceful place. A special place. Joey looked down at the jagged rocks below. Shimmering sea glass, scattered around the rocks, sparkled from the sun. "Diamonds in the rough," Joey thought. Her mind turned to the little girl who had died on the ship with her parents. She could understand her anger—unwillingly separated from her parents, desperately wishing she could be reunited with them. Joey certainly knew how that felt. When Joey's mom died, she couldn't imagine life without her. Whether it was making breakfast together on Sunday mornings or reading chapters from *Little Women* at night before bed, her absence left a void in Joey's life that could never be filled.

Her mind drifted to her father. He had also left a gaping hole in her life. Having a convict as your father didn't exactly make you proud to be "Daddy's little girl." But when he was released from prison, Joey was able to put all those feelings aside. Sure, she'd had fears about him coming back into her life, but when he did, she was grateful to be reunited. When he was sent back to prison for the second time, it nearly killed her.

Her shoulder was getting sore, so she switched her backpack to her other shoulder.

"Jo-sephine . . ." a voice hummed through the air. It was the same voice she had heard murmuring within the wallpaper. Joey looked along the beach nervously and checked the cliff. There was no one in sight. Trusting that it was just her low blood sugar, Joey took out her chocolate bar from her lunch sack and glanced at her watch. She was right on time. But where were the other interns? Where was Kate? They were all supposed to meet at the lighthouse for a quick tour.

Maybe they're already at the lighthouse, she thought. But before she could call out to them—

"Play with me Jo-sephine . . . play with me . . ." the bewitching voice called. Joey looked around frantically. No one was around.

"Play with me Jo-sephine . . . play with me . . ." the voice demanded. It sounded like a heartbroken melody on a music box.

"Play with me Jo-sephine . . . play with me . . ." The sound seemed to come from all around Joey. It was in the waves, and on the beach. And it wouldn't stop. Mist blew around Joey and she felt trapped. She desperately tried to slap it away. She couldn't. Terrified, Joey raced to Manor Light and rushed inside. She slammed the lighthouse door behind her and the voice instantly ceased.

The first floor of the lighthouse was like an icebox. Frightened and freezing, Joey took a navy blue windbreaker out of her backpack and pulled it over her head. Shivering, she glanced up to the watchtower. "Hello?" her voice quavered. "Hello, hello, hello, hello, hello . . ." Joey listened to her voice echo up the spiral staircase. She prayed for a response. There was none. Joey looked around the circular room. It was dark and musty. Suddenly, a strong force pushed Joey toward the stairs. She found herself with one foot balanced on the first step of the staircase. A child's fragile laughter sounded from the stones around her. Joey bolted.

Racing out of the lighthouse as fast as she could, Joey ran down the cliff and down across the beach. The unearthly chant followed her all the way.

"Play with me Jo-sephine . . . play with me . . ." the voice laughed.

Joey stopped near the waves. She'd had enough. She stomped her feet on the wet sand.

"Stop it. Stop it, now," Joey commanded. The beckoning voice filtered away. Joey took a deep breath, then sighed in relief. Exhausted, she dropped to the sand and sat down. Joey shut her eyes. She could feel her heart pounding. Something had scared her. As she sat there, she convinced herself the noise had just been the wind playing tricks on her mind. Calmed by the heavy surf against the sand, Joey opened her eyes.

Glancing around at the empty beach, she was struck with a sense of loss that grew and grew. Even after her mom's death, she had never felt such dark despair. A bitter taste rose in her mouth. Her hands turned icy. She felt like crying but her eyes were too heavy for tears. The feeling pressed, until she noticed . . . In front of her! What was that? Joey's heart leaped. Small footprints were racing around her in the sand. Joey turned her head, watching the tiny dancing tracks circling her. An English girl's sweet voice brushed against her ear.

"I'm sorry I frightened you . . ." she offered to Joey, sincerely.

"Is someone there?" Joey asked, not really expecting an answer.

"Yes. It's me, Mary. Mary Breckinridge . . ." the voice responded. Joey looked around her, terrified. No one was there. She was all alone, but for the tracks of tiny footprints in the sand. And very slowly, even those faded away.

Jen looked at Pacey, lying under a huge oak tree, while she toiled with an old pair of yellow rubber overalls Gramps had used for fly-fishing. After half a day working with Pacey at the aquarium, Jen was ready to call it quits. She knew Pacey had serious slacker tendencies during the school year, but during the summer he was a slacker personified. So far, he had spent the entire day watching and napping. Jen sighed, and then pulled the oversize pants up around her waist and looped her arms under the suspenders. If Abby Morgan were alive, she would definitely call this a fashion don't.

"Sexy, Lindley," Pacey yelled from his spot beneath the tree. "Some people find rubber to be a real turn-on."

Jen squinted her eyes to look at him. The sun was already beating down hard. "Pacey, are you going to do anything this summer besides masquerade as the not-so-witty Greek Chorus?"

Pacey looked taken aback. "Whose bed did you wake up on the wrong side of?"

Jen threw down her bucket. "My own, Pacey. And while I might not be turning cartwheels at the thought of our summer internship, at least I'm trying my best. And it's really annoying to have you sit on your lazy butt giving a running commentary of the 'Top 25 movie stars under 25'!"

Pacey looked up from his magazine, hurt for a second. "Look, I'd rather not read about them either. But Kate doesn't keep *Playboy* on the coffee table."

"Okay, Pacey. Slack off all you want. I don't care," Jen said in exasperation.

Pacey smiled, "C'mon, Lindley, what do you expect? It's summer vacation!"

Jen sighed as she picked up the bucket to continue her chores. She might not have been the go-getter like Dawson or a straight-A student like Joey, but she had moved past her New York self-destructive days. Sleeping until noon and coming home whenever she pleased had only provided her parents with a "tough-love" excuse for an invitation to live with Grams. Two years later, Jen knew it was the best thing that had ever happened to her. And now, she was determined to prove, not only to her parents, but also to herself, that she was so much more than that troubled girl from New York. She was responsible, she was determined, she was . . . sick of Pacey.

There was no denying it—Jen's success at her internship, and mental sanity, depended on getting Pacey to actually do some work. She glanced over at Pacey, bored under the tree. It wasn't that Pacey didn't care, he just wasn't very inspired. Jen had an idea.

"Far be it from me to remind you of the video cameras in here monitoring our every move, Pacey," Jen hinted, setting her trap. Pacey sat up and looked around the aquarium, noticing Big Brother's electronic eyes.

"So what if someone catches me falling asleep on the job. What's the worst that can happen? They fire me?" Pacey asked.

"But do you really want to risk losing your chance with Kate?" Jen queried.

"What's that supposed to mean?" Pacey questioned, curious.

"Nothing, really. I just thought she seemed kind of into you yesterday," Jen mused.

"You think?" Pacey asked, excited.

"Duh . . . ," Jen encouraged, continuing. "She kept staring at you with her intense blue eyes, she twirled her red hair every time she laughed at one of your jokes, and let's not forget her weird obsession in getting back at your brother Dougie for ditching her at the prom."

Pacey stood up and picked up a bucket. "Maybe I'll go play with Abigail for a while," he muttered, trying to act cool.

"Fine, and while you're at it, throw her some herring. Maybe that will stop her from making that whining noise."

Pacey walked toward Abigail's pool. "It's whistling,

Jen. Dolphins whistle. And, no, I won't feed Abigail any more fish. She eats more in a day than Leery's Fresh Fish serves in a week. We keep feeding that dolphin too much herring and she's gonna outgrow her pool."

"I don't care. Whistling or whining. Whatever you want to call it, it's been getting on my nerves. Just feed her," Jen demanded, as she walked down toward the beach to scavenge for seashells. She was happy that she solved her problem with Pacey. If only she had been given the lighthouse internship. So what if it was haunted. She'd much rather give tours, instead of, once again, standing up to her knees in salt water smelling like fish. She looked at her watch. At least it was almost lunchtime.

When Dawson appeared at the car at lunchtime, Joey had already been sitting in it for over an hour. Dawson grabbed a large picnic basket from the backseat. He looked at Joey curiously, "You been waiting long, Joe?" Joey shrugged.

"A while," she muttered softly.

Dawson glanced sideways at her. "Any particular reason?"

Joey looked over at Dawson, suspiciously. "What particular reason would I have?" Dawson gave Joey a knowing glance.

"There are no such things as haunted lighthouses and spooky ghosts," Dawson confirmed.

Joey took a deep breath. "Tell that to Mary Breckinridge," she declared. Trying to remain calm, Dawson joined Joey in the car. Joey went on to recount the events—the haunting voice in the wall-paper, the same haunting voice she heard on the beach and in the lighthouse, the ghostly footprints in the sand. For a moment, Dawson was speech-less.

"But what makes you think it's the ghost of Mary Breckinridge?" Dawson posed.

"She *told* me," Joey responded, scanning his face. He didn't believe her!

Dawson had a weird look on his face. He was thinking of Nick and the Breckinridge ship. *How would Joey know the little girl's name? She must have read the name in the tour guide pamphlet and filed it away in her subconscious,* Dawson thought to himself. *Yes, that had to be it.* Dawson tried to reason with her. "Joey, wallpaper doesn't speak and a little girl's footprints don't just sud-denly appear and disappear in the sand."

Joey looked at Dawson. A week ago, she might have agreed. But today, she wasn't so sure. "I know what you're thinking. I'm not crazy," Joey stated.

"We all let our imaginations run wild at times, Joey. That's the beauty of having one," Dawson tried. Joey smiled. She could always count on Dawson to turn something negative into something positive.

"Thanks Dawson," Joey said, comforted.

"C'mon, Joey," Dawson urged. He grabbed the picnic basket. "Jen and Pacey are waiting for us to bring them lunch." Dawson climbed out of the SUV. Although hesitant, Joey decided to join him.

But if she was going to make it through her internship, she knew her wild imagination was something she was going to have to control.

Joey and Dawson walked into the aquarium. Pacey, thinking it was Kate, jumped up, pretending to help Jen. When he realized it was Joey, he made a face. "Potter," he said. "Try knocking next time." He picked up his *People* magazine. "You made me lose my place." Joey's eyes penetrated right through him. "What's the matter, Potter?" Pacey asked. "Getting lonely up there on the bluff?"

Dawson sighed at Pacey. "I bet you haven't left that spot all day."

Jen, disgusted by handling live fish, looked over. "I can vouch for that," she said. Jen threw the last of the lunch to a bunch of barking harbor seals. She walked over to interact with Abigail.

Joey frowned. "I'm in a crappy, damp lighthouse while you get to play with a cute dolphin? Life just isn't fair."

"Actually, it's pretty crappy and damp in here, too," Jen said. Getting increasingly worked up, she continued, "I mean, one minute I'm relaxing, enjoying my summer, and the next minute I'm slinging fish, getting barked at by seals, pissing off a Flipper look-alike, and dreaming about *Jaws*—"

"You want to switch jobs?" Joey asked.

"You want to be tormented by a temperamental dolphin?" Jen questioned, in disbelief.

"Oh, Lindley," Pacey laughed. "You're just bitter Shamu doesn't like you."

"Shamu was a killer whale, you toad," Jen said, deadpan.

Pacey clapped his hands together, jumping to his feet. "Watch and learn, Lindley," he said, enthusiastically. Pacey stepped up to the side of the pool. Hoping Kate was watching him from her office, he winked at the video camera somewhere overhead. The dolphin swam over. Pacey did different hand motions and, surprisingly, Abigail responded. She jumped, flipped, and even floated across the water. Pacey leaned over the pool and Abigail swam over to him, belly-side up. Pacey leaned down and rubbed her belly. Joey, Jen, and Dawson were floored. Kate, who was watching from her office, was impressed as well.

"How on earth do you know what you're doing?" Joey asked Pacey in amazement.

"The Witter family used the same techniques to train me," Pacey said with a wink. Dawson, Joey, and Jen exchanged glances. Sadly, it was probably true. Meanwhile, the dolphin stopped performing. Abigail had been doing trick after trick and was now waiting patiently for her reward. Jen was standing near the bucket of dolphin food—defrosting, nostril-flaring fish.

"Lindley," Pacey begged, "I need a hand here."

Jen glanced at the bucket. No way. She smiled. "Do what you usually do, Pacey. Use your own." Joey and Dawson laughed. Jen could hold her own with the quick insults. Although not particularly close, Joey thought of Jen as her best girlfriend kind of by default. There was Andie, who was away on vacation with Jack, but Joey had known Jen longer. Andie was someone Joey understood. Jen was the type of person, at one time or another, Joey wanted to be. She could remember how Dawson looked at Jen when she stepped out of the cab before tenth grade. Joey had waited so long for Dawson to look at her that way. Joey glanced over to Dawson. He was finally looking at her *that way*. Why wasn't she responsive?

"Because you want to spend your time with me," Mary Breckinridge's voice tickled in Joey's ear. Joey jumped, a bit frightened. The voice had followed her into the aquarium. Joey glanced around the room, feeling paranoid. Dawson, Jen, and Pacey had not heard it. But to Joey, the voice was as distinct as her own. *Maybe that was it!* Joey thought to herself. Maybe this was just a voice in her head. She frowned, unsure which was worse—being haunted or becoming a mental case study. After half-a-second of pondering, Joey chose mental case. The voice of Mary Breckinridge was really just the voice of her own inner child elbowing its way past her adult's constant financial, educational, and personal struggles and fears. She had wanted a summer of mindless fun. Maybe if she listened to the voice she'd have one. But just as Joey had decided she was projecting . . .

"Albeit, he is a handsome lad," the voice continued, referring to Dawson. Okay, Joey thought, if this voice of hers wanted to check out Dawson Leery's blond good looks, who was she to complain?

"Be my best chum, Josephine," the voice urged. Despite her rationalization, Joey looked around the aquarium for a sign of her. She imagined what Mary might look like.

"Blond hair, brown hair, blue eyes, gray eyes . . . Play with me, Josephine. I'll show you what I look like," Mary tempted. Despite the fear, Joey looked around the room, intrigued.

"Joey? Joey? Earth to Joey!" Jen shouted.

Snapping out of her dream, Joey glanced over to the pool. Abigail had tired of Pacey's rewardless tricks. Using her tail, she had gently knocked him into the pool. As Pacey pulled himself out of the water, Dawson pulled out his video camera and started filming.

"I'm going to have to keep this on at all times, or I might miss something," Dawson laughed. He filmed Pacey standing on the side of the pool.

"I . . . think . . . I . . . have . . . the . . . hiccups," Pacey managed between spitting out large gulps of water. Dawson turned his camera on Abigail. The dolphin was innocently looking at them from the far end of the pool.

"And what do you have to say about all this?" Dawson asked the dolphin. If there was such a thing as a dolphin wink, Abigail did it that day.

Jen walked over and peered into the bucket with a shudder. "Now *that*," she said, "deserves a reward." She threw a fish to Abigail, who happily swam over to receive it. Everyone started snickering, which turned into the kind of bellyaching laugh that makes the stomach muscles feel like they've done two hundred sit-ups. Dawson set his camera down. Jen offered Pacey her extra pair of rubber pants. Joey looked around the room and smiled. She thought she could hear Mary laughing, too.

Strangely, Abigail didn't join in their fun. Instead, she had turned her attention to Joey. Dawson, Pacey, and Jen noticed the dolphin's odd stare.

"What?" Joey asked, self-conscious. Abigail backed up in the pool away from Joey.

"She's frightened of you," Pacey stated to Joey.

"No, she's not," Joey protested. Abigail started making odd noises as she splashed around the pool.

"Yeah, she is scared of you, Joey," Jen agreed, a bit freaked. Their fun moment interrupted, Joey felt a coldness all around her.

"You guys, stop it," Joey urged. "She's just a dolphin."

Dawson turned off his video camera and packed it back into its case. "C'mon, Joey. Let's get out of here," he urged.

If Dawson had looked through the viewfinder, he would have realized why the dolphin was acting so strangely. Captured on film was an image. It was of

Mary. But she wasn't the beautiful, shimmering soul Joey had imagined. She was a little English girl—her gray face was bloated, her long blond hair was matted with seaweed, her white dress was tattered with blood and sand, and her cold, terrified eyes stared intently at Joey.

4

X Marks the Spot

Joey smiled. Dawson rolled up on his black mountain bike to greet Joey. "This cliff really bites," he complained, hot and sweaty. It was early in the morning, but the summer sun was already hammering down.

"How'd it go?" Dawson asked.

She had just completed her first official Manor Light tour. And after a week of giving up Dawson's reinstated movie nights to memorize her tour guide speech, she was well prepared to recite information and answer questions. One guy had even asked her for her phone number. She hadn't given it to him, of course, but she was flattered that people seemed to enjoy the tour. One family even asked her to pose for a picture with them.

In her first tour there had been six people. She eagerly answered many of their questions, even adding some of her own research to make the tour more interesting. Joey was amazed at the number of people who visited Woodland Beach to tour Manor Light. With three tours per day averaging five to fifteen people per tour, Joey would welcome fifteen to forty-five people a day into her creepy lighthouse.

"Really well, thanks," Joey replied, handing Dawson a bottle of water from her bright red backpack.

"No more mysterious voices?" he asked, tentatively.

"Nope," Joey said. All week long Dawson had been pushing her to talk about Mary Breckinridge, but she didn't want to.

Dawson continued, "So, it's safe to say your imagination's no longer running away with you?"

"With all this training, I think my imagination has come to an abrupt halt," Joey complained.

Dawson nodded, "Yeah, I'm glad to be finished with orientation-week-from-hell as well. We've got summer movies to get back to."

Joey nodded, distracted. Truth was, she hadn't heard from Mary in a week, but that hadn't stopped Joey from thinking about the voice or listening for it every day. All week, she had wrestled with why her inner child had jumped to the front of her mind. And with no clear answers, she was still wondering what had made it materialize. "Well, my next tour is in thirty minutes and I need to practice," Joey explained, as she walked away.

"How about lunch afterward?" Dawson called after her. "I'll be down on the dock," he added.

"The dock?" Joey questioned, turning around. They had been eating lunch with Pacey and Jen at the aquarium the last couple of days.

Dawson frowned. "Nick thinks he has a lead. He wants us to go out for a quick tour of the inlet right after lunch."

"Hmmm . . ." Joey looked at her watch, deciding. She thought about the aquarium and how Abigail had yet to warm to her. Joey couldn't understand why. Animals always loved her.

"See ya at the dock, then," Dawson said, not giving Joey a chance to say no. Pedaling away on his bike, he added, "Good luck on your next tour."

"Thanks, Dawson," she smiled, as she walked off in the other direction. She was excited to finally meet Nick. It was suspicious that Dawson had yet to introduce him. Listening to other interns gossip, though, Joey guessed Nick was quite a hunk. A tall, dark and handsome hunk. Joey looked down at her tour guide uniform—white shorts and navy blue polo shirt. She opened up her backpack to check what "civilian clothes" she had hurriedly packed that morning. Joey frowned. All she had were cut-off jean shorts and a faded Ice-House T-shirt. She sighed. *No, no, no,* Joey thought to herself. She did not want to be the kind of girl to obsess about her appearance. "Talent and attitude—that's what counts," Joey insisted to herself. She slouched her shoulders, discouraged. As of late, she had stopped working on her talent and her attitude had been rather depressed. Well, maybe a little flirtation would get her out of her head.

Twenty minutes later, Dawson was wandering through stacks of books at the Taylor Museum, writing down card catalog numbers and struggling to remember the Dewey decimal system. The room was cold from the large window air-conditioner. Its loud humming gently rocked a few nearby readers to sleep. But not Dawson. He anxiously sought a lead to confirm that the Breckinridge shipwreck happened and the wreck existed.

After two hours of searching, Dawson sat down at a table, discouraged. He could find no lead. He was beginning to doubt if there had ever been a ship, a Breckinridge family, or a crash upon the rocks. Nick had found his story in a legend book, not a history book. His thesis was based on hearsay, not fact. Nick was supposed to be a scientist, but basing an underwater deep-sea dive on a legend didn't sound very scientific to Dawson. Dawson opened his spiral notebook and jotted down his concerns: a mysterious beacon failing to signal its light; a foghorn that may or may not have been a mermaid; an angry little girl haunting the lighthouse. *Yeah, right.* . . . Dawson closed his notebook. He was absolutely convinced Nick's legend was just like any other legend—a fairy tale.

"What's the problem, Leery?" a familiar voice questioned. Dawson looked over to see Jen sitting at a table. She was surrounded by books and doing a little research of her own. Dawson walked over and joined her.

"Filming Nick in his temporary office isn't the cinematic achievement I'd hoped for this summer," Dawson confessed. Curious, he sat down next to Jen. "What are you doing here?" he asked.

Jen sighed, "Trying to solve a little problem of my own." Dawson scanned the wide array of books surrounding Jen. He picked one up, and his eyes widened.

"*Dolphins and Death*," he read off one of the spines. "You aren't planning some twisted, illegal plot, are you?" Dawson interrogated. Jen grabbed the book out of Dawson's hand.

"It's not what you think. If I was going to murder any large mammal, it would be Pacey," Jen assured.

"So what's with all the books?" Dawson asked.

"It's Abigail," Jen said. "She'll happily entertain anybody but me. Pacey even went swimming with her yesterday. But all she does is torment me," Jen sighed. She added, "And I control her treats!"

"How can a cute little dolphin torment you?" Dawson questioned, in disbelief.

"Cute? Little?" Jen gasped. "You'd be surprised. When I try to feed her, she goes for my hand."

"Maybe you're not feeding her enough?" Dawson

said. "I mean, she's not used to being kept in captivity. She's used to catching her own food."

"Not feeding her enough?" Jen gasped. "She eats more times a day than I do. You'd think she was eating for two." Jen looked up, curious. Maybe it wasn't more than just a little hormones, causing Abigail to remain constantly cranky. Jen quickly flipped through the pages of her book. Taking his exit, Dawson got up from the table.

"Well, if you'll excuse me," he said, "I'll be going back to my own mystery." Jen glanced up from her book.

"Looking up creepy facts on Joey's haunted lighthouse?" she teased.

"Not exactly," answered Dawson. "I'm trying to find information on the Breckinridge shipwreck," he advised.

"And . . ." Jen pressed.

Dawson sat down to explain. "Well, I'm beginning to wonder if there ever was a ship."

"Why's that?" Jen asked, not really all that interested.

"For one, the only source of the wreckage story, *The Lightwatchman's Journal*, is suspicious."

"How's that?" Jen uttered, not really listening. She turned her attention back to her book. Dawson didn't mind. He was pleased to have an excuse to work out his problem out loud.

"The guy had a heavy drinking problem," Dawson stated.

"Locked up in a lighthouse with no TV or

Twinkies . . . I'd have a drinking problem too," Jen laughed. Dawson ignored Jen's commentary.

"The Breckinridge ship was sailing from England to Cape Cod. One would think a port in England would've logged its departure, right? But no one did," Dawson smugly answered his own question.

"And . . ." Jen said, turning another page of her book.

"And the supposed body of Mary Breckinridge, the only body to be recovered from the wreckage . . ." Dawson continued, ". . . was conveniently buried in an undisclosed grave."

"No valid account. No ship. No victims. Nick has you digging for a buried treasure without an 'X' that marks the spot," Jen concluded, without ever looking up from her book.

"Precisely," Dawson gloomily agreed.

Joey grabbed her backpack and headed down to the beach to meet Dawson for lunch. She decided to wait beneath a huge oak tree. She sat, her back against the trunk, and smiled appreciatively up at the large shady leaves. Joey took her lunch out of her backpack and opened the paper bag. "Peanut butter and jelly again," she said to herself. Dawson approached, laughing at her disgust.

"Wanna trade?" Dawson asked. "I've got leftovers from the restaurant."

"Thanks for the offer, but I can deal," Joey responded. "It's just, you'd think with a gourmet cook on hand at the B&B, Bessie could get a little more creative with lunch." Joey took a bite out of her sandwich as Nick approached. Joey squinted at him, into the sun. He was incredibly handsome and before she knew it, he was standing above her, hand extended. Joey shook it.

"You must be the Joey that I've been hearing so much about," Nick teased. Nick's voice was rough like his hands.

Joey coughed, then croaked out, "Really?" She smiled. "All good things, I hope." Nick smiled back. He took a seat beside Joey, as she quickly wiped a dab of peanut butter off the corner of her mouth.

"Looks tasty," he observed.

Joey held up her sandwich, blushing, "PBJ."

Nick nodded, "My favorite!" Joey took out the other half of her sandwich.

"Here, have half," she offered.

Nick raised his eyebrows, "You sure?" Joey smiled and handed him half. He held up his half. "Cheers!" They pretended to "clink" their sandwiches together, then each took a bite.

Meanwhile, Dawson sat nearby, pushing his pasta around his Tupperware container with a small plastic fork. He looked back and forth between Joey and Nick. He wasn't sure where their flirtation was going, but he was pretty sure he didn't like it.

"So," Joey asked Nick, "Dawson says you're working on your thesis?"

"Yeah." Nick finished chewing. "It's been going well so far. But it would be better if we could raise that ship. . . . Right, Dawson?" Dawson looked up from his lunch.

"Yeah, whatever," he mumbled. Joey shot Dawson a look, as Nick got an idea.

"Hey, Joey. Maybe you'd like to help us?" he asked.

Before Joey could answer, Dawson jumped in, "She's giving tours at the lighthouse. Time-consuming, in-depth tours."

"Not that time-consuming," Joey argued. This seemed perfect. She could kill two birds with one stone. Three, actually. Not only could she hang out with Nick and be doing something exciting and fun, she could also spend less time in the lighthouse. "I mean," Joey continued, "I could talk to Kate about it. I could tell her you could use another set of hands."

"I think two sets is enough," Dawson muttered as he closed his Tupperware container, pasta only half-eaten. "I'm going to get back to work." Nick stood up.

"Good idea, Dawson. That ship won't raise itself." Nick turned to Joey and smiled, "Nice to meet you, Joey."

"You too," Joey smiled. Joey zipped up her backpack to leave, but decided to wait. It was thirty minutes until her next tour, and she was going to enjoy it. Lying back against the tree, she watched Dawson and Nick walk down to the dock. Nick looked different from most of the guys she had known. Tall, slender, and with glittering green eyes, he held a worldly mysteriousness that the boys in Capeside sorely missed. He was confident, but not smooth. And his thick, dark hair was tousled about in a cute, in-need-of-a-haircut kind of way. Yes, she was definitely going to talk to Kate about helping Nick.

Thirty minutes later, Joey walked up the cliff toward the lighthouse to begin her next tour. She turned to watch Dawson and Nick motor out into the ocean. She hoped they would be okay. The Woodland Beach research vessel looked as old as Woodland Beach itself. It was similar to a Coast Guard cutter, but not as shiny and new. Joey watched the waves break around the boat as the engine picked up speed. She waved good-bye to them both. Nick waved back. Dawson pretended not to notice her farewell. Continuing on, Joey sighed. Dawson hadn't seemed too happy about Nick and her hitting it off so well. Joey saw the look Dawson gave her when she smiled at Nick. Joey knew that look well.

It was the very same look she gave him when Jen first came to Capeside and Dawson was completely tongue-tied at the sight of her. That look had been thrown back and forth between the two of them like a ball that never stopped bouncing. She supposed one day it would stop—either when they grew up and moved on or when they found their way back to each other. But right now, they weren't together and Nick had definitely piqued her interest.

Back at the lighthouse, Joey walked out to the end of the cliff, to take one last look at the guys venturing out to sea. The boat had become a tiny speck in the ocean. Joey's glance swept over the shore. A figure caught her eye. A little girl was standing on the beach near the oak tree—the same spot where Joey had just been sitting for lunch. The little girl was odd, dressed differently from most children her age. She looked about eight years old. She had very fair skin and long wavy blond hair. She wore an all white dress with lots of buttons. Her boots were black leather with hooks and laces. A large woven hat hung low over her face. The hat was made of a light-colored straw, with little white flowers embroidered along the rim. She looked as though she had stepped out from the past. Joey hesitated. Could it be her whispering ghost, Mary? Frightened, Joey squeezed her eyes shut, then opened them again, expecting her to be gone. But the little girl still stood there firmly, arms on her hips, staring at Joey.

Joey shifted, not knowing what to do. For what seemed like an entire day, Joey stood there gazing at the Victorian child as if soaking in a watercolor painting. Finally, the little girl smiled, lifted her arm and pointed toward the oak tree. Her posture was adamant. Certain the girl was trying to tell her something, Joey ran down to the beach. The closer she came to the child, the more Joey was sure it was Mary. She just knew it. The figure had an unearthly quality—a Sleeping Beauty magic. When Joey neared the beach, the little girl walked around behind the oak tree and, as quickly as she had appeared, she disappeared. Joey was in disbelief. Where had Mary gone? Joey walked over to the tree and glanced behind it. There was no little girl. Walking back around, she noticed something sparkling on the ground. She walked over and saw that it was her wallet, its metal zipper glinting in the sun. She had dropped her wallet while sitting under the tree. That's what the little girl had been trying to tell her. It must have fallen out of her backpack when she stood to up to leave after lunch.

As Joey picked up her wallet, she noticed some-thing else—something that had definitely not been there before. A huge "X" was carved into the trunk of the tree. Joey studied the letter emblazoned in the bark. Its length and width were rather large, the incision quite deep. She placed her hand against it. The tree felt warm. The "X" was perfectly shaped, almost as if it had been branded into the tree.

When Dawson and Nick sailed back in, Joey was waiting for them at the dock. Dawson hopped off the boat. "Joe, what is it?" he asked, concerned. Joey took a moment, afraid to answer. If she said it out loud, it would make her haunting or insanity true.

"It's Mary," she whispered. Dawson sighed. Maybe he should just offer to trade with her now—she could work with Nick and he'd take over her lighthouse duties. "Dawson," Joey tried to explain. "It's not just the voice anymore. Something else happened." Dawson raised his eyebrows, waiting for her to explain. "I saw her," Joey confessed. Nick walked up and stood with Joey and Dawson.

"Who?" he asked, interrupting.

"If you wouldn't mind, Nick, this is private," Dawson said. Nick looked over at Joey, ignoring Dawson.

"Are you sure?" Nick questioned. Joey nodded her head "yes." Nick turned to leave, saying, "Okay, but don't forget to talk to Kate about helping me out with my research."

"I won't," Joey promised, smitten. Dawson was irritated.

"Okay, Romeo, that's enough," he said.

Nick eyed Dawson thoughtfully. "I'll leave you guys to talk," he said, departing. Dawson walked over to Joey and placed his arm around her shoulder.

"Okay, explain," he encouraged her.

"I saw a little girl," Joey whispered up to him. "It was Mary."

"There are tons of people who come to Woodland Beach to tour Manor Light, Joey. And that includes little girls," Dawson comforted.

"Well, this little girl wasn't at the lighthouse,"

Joey explained. "She was by the oak tree where we ate lunch today."

"Did you talk to her?" Dawson questioned.

"Not exactly. But she motioned me to come back to the tree. And when I did, I found my wallet lying on the ground," Joey explained.

"Let me get this straight. A girl found your wallet and pointed it out to you—and it makes her the ghost of Mary Breckinridge. How?" Dawson asked loudly.

"Because there was an 'X' marked in the tree trunk," Joey hollered back, angered at Dawson's impatience.

Dawson exploded. "Joey," he said urgently, "stop it, okay? Not only is this interfering with your job, it's jeopardizing your sanity. It's a lighthouse. Not a mysterious, creepy, haunted lighthouse. But a regular, old, historical lighthouse . . . that's all!"

"Why don't you just admit what's really bothering you?" Joey shot back.

"You want permission to hang all over my coworker? Fine, permission granted," Dawson snapped.

"Nick and I just met, " Joey said. "I was just being friendly."

"Like you and I are friendly?" Dawson waited anxiously for her response. Joey practically laughed at his question.

"Sure, Dawson," she said sarcastically. "I can really compare a guy I met three hours ago with someone I've been watching movies with for the last seventeen years."

"Watching movies?" Dawson asked, hurt. "Is that all we did?"

"No." Joey was getting frazzled. "That's not what I meant. Why are you twisting around everything I'm saying?"

"Fine, then let me be very clear. . . ." Joey waited as Dawson searched for the right words. The fact was that he was jealous. He didn't like the idea of Joey with anyone else. Why couldn't he just admit it to her? "I'd just prefer it," Dawson said, chickening out, "if you would stick to your own internship." Joey looked at him, shocked. She didn't know what to say to him. She shook her head and angrily walked off toward the lighthouse.

At the top of the cliff, Joey glanced down at Dawson still standing by the shore. Dawson looked up at Joey. He loved her big brown eyes and classic Joey Potter half-smile, but if he could have made out her expression, he was sure it would be an angry scowl. Dawson glanced down at his feet, confused. He didn't want to hurt Joey. He loved her. Yet, he couldn't stand the thought of her and Nick flirting all summer long. Nick probably had a first love, a soul mate. Maybe he could get Nick to empathize with him and steer clear of Joey. Yes. Dawson would take the problem out of Joey's hands and put it into Nick's. Dawson glanced up to the cliff, hoping to shout an apology . . . but Joey had already left.

* * *

Dawson found Jen in the museum, still sitting at her table. He walked over to her, and rested his hand on her large stack of research. He stared at her for a long moment, reminded of the conversation he'd had with her earlier in the morning—something about buried treasure and . . . "Would you like to join me in a match of tic-tac-toe? You take the 'X's' and I'll take the 'O's'," Dawson said. Jen glanced up at Dawson as though he were insane.

"Sure thing, Dawson. Right after I play Pacey in a game of hopscotch."

"So whose idea was the stupid prank?" Dawson continued, getting right to the point. "Yours or Pacey's?" Jen had no idea what he was talking about or where his hostility was coming from.

"Do you want to explain yourself?" she asked.

"The 'X' on the tree . . . very clever. Joey is delusional enough about this lighthouse without your encouragement. And I'm actually surprised. I thought you had a change of heart about the internship and planned to take it seriously." Jen couldn't believe what she was hearing. Dawson was yelling at her for something and she had no idea what.

"You don't know what you're talking about, Dawson." Jen picked up her books to leave. "And Joey's not the only one who's delusional." Jen stormed out of the museum as angrily as Dawson had stormed in. "Get a grip," she snapped, wondering what the heck his problem was. Dawson watched Jen exit, shame setting in. However coincidental, he knew she didn't have anything to do with the marking on the tree. Jen was all for practical jokes, but this one wasn't her style. It was way too mean and way too time-consuming. Dawson sighed; he now had two women to apologize to. Noticing Dawson wallowing in gloom, Nick approached.

"What's up, Leery?" Nick asked, more of a statement than a question.

"How's it going with you?" Dawson shot back. A question answered with a question? In guy terms this meant a standoff. Nick looked at Dawson and threw a third comment into the mix.

"You tell me." Nick stared at Dawson. It was the kind of stare that said it all. There was no need for Dawson to have a heart-to-heart with Nick about the sanctity of soul mates. Nope. Nick was going to pursue Joey. And Dawson would just have to deal.

Jen, fuming, walked toward the aquarium. She hated always being the scapegoat. Every time something went wrong in Capeside, Jen Lindley was the bad girl to blame. A stolen test—Jen took it. Someone drunk—must be Jen. Getting it on underneath the sheets—Ding! Ding! Ding!— Jennifer's the winner. Sometimes, Jen simply hated her name. "Jeenniiffeerr!" While she loved her Grams dearly, she cringed at the way she pronounced her name as if every letter was doubled. When Jen was little, her favorite costume was a pink wig, white go-go boots, and a tambourine.

Wanting to be a rock star, she had demanded her parents call her 'Bubbles.' Older and wiser, she was grateful her parents had refused. But sometimes she couldn't help but wonder . . . would she have grown up to be a different person had her name not been one she'd hated!?

"If it isn't . . . the one . . . the only . . . the Jjeenniiffeerr Lliinnddlleeyy . . ." Pacey clapped and cheered as Jen walked into the aquarium.

"Don't start with me, Pacey," Jen stressed. "I've had a long day."

"So have I." Pacey sat down at the edge of the pool. "All this hard work, and I'm getting nowhere with Kate," he explained. Abigail swam up to Pacey and tucked her head in his lap, sympathetic.

Jen came over, slipped off her tennis shoes, and sat down beside Pacey. Dipping her feet into the water, she reached over to pat the dolphin's head. Abigail ducked back under the water and began circling the pool. Jen frowned. The dolphin still didn't want to be around her. Jen twinkled her toes across the shimmering surface. The pool wasn't the crystal blue water it normally was. "What's with the odd green color?" Jen observed.

"Kate came in earlier and did a bunch of tests. Some kind of chemical imbalance thingy," Pacey answered. Jen frowned. From the research she had done earlier, she knew that could mean trouble. She hoped it was the water mineral causing the problem and not Abigail's health.

"So, what did you do all day?" Pacey asked. Jen

continued to stare at Abigail. Abigail stopped circling the pool and met Jen's gaze.

"Research. Abigail's pregnant."

"I knew those two barking seals were trouble," Pacey teased. Jen frowned.

"Pacey, I'm serious," Jen stated.

"Sure, Lindley," Pacey stood up, smiling. "Am I supposed to believe that one of the tests Kate ran today contained a little strip with a blue box and a pink box?"

"She's pregnant, Pacey, and according to Kate, due in two weeks and if what I've just read is true, she's not big enough, or strong enough, to deliver a three foot long calf." Jen stood up, worried.

"You really did do research today," Pacey said, impressed. Jen walked over, picked up her books and brought them over to the side of the pool.

"And obviously, I'm going to need to do a little more." Jen sat back down on the side of the pool and stuck her feet back into the water. Pacey frowned.

"Does this new mothering instinct of yours mean I'm getting stuck with the seals?" Pacey questioned. Meanwhile, Abigail had stopped circling the pool. She swam over to Jen and rested beside her. Jen waited. Abigail nudged her toe. Jen smiled, triumphant. Somehow, she had won the dolphin over. At least for now.

Nick found Joey outside the lighthouse. She was sitting on a bench, taking deep breaths. "It's just a lighthouse. It's just a lighthouse. It's just a lighthouse," she whispered to herself. Joey had finished her last lighthouse tour of the day in record time. She changed into her civilian clothes, ready to go home, but she wasn't ready to face her friends. With an hour to kill, she decided to sit on the cliff. Part of Joey was hoping her ghost friend Mary would come back to visit and explain to her the rules of being haunted. Nick sat down beside Joey.

"Want to tell me what's going on?" he questioned. Normally, Joey would have been ecstatic to have a guy like Nick sitting next to her. Besides being tall, dark, and handsome, he was smart, outdoorsy, and funny. But right now, Joey didn't even look twice at him. He could have been the Elephant Man for all she cared.

Nick asked again, "What's going on, Joey?" Was there any point in Joey explaining herself? Pacey had laughed at her, Jen didn't care, and Dawson had looked at her like she was telling him the sky was green and the grass was blue. Was Nick going to react any differently?

"Nothing, really," she lied.

"Joey, I might not know you that well, but I can sure tell something is bothering you."

"You're going to think I'm totally crazy," she said.

"Give me a try," Nick said. He picked a perfect seaside rose off the blooming bush behind them and gave it to Joey. Joey smelled its sweet scent, and then sneezed.

"Terrible allergies," she explained, embarrassed,

Nick took the flower back. As he held it in his hand, he smelled the scent—and sneezed too. They shared a laugh. Joey unzipped her backpack and pulled out some tissues. She handed one to Nick and took one for herself. "Roses are a favorite of mine," Joey smiled.

"You don't have to say that, Joey," Nick comforted.

"No, really," Joey insisted. "We have lots of them around the house where I live. I used to argue with my mom, before she died, that when I got married and had a house of my own I was going have them in every room in my house, every day of the week. Mom insisted that I couldn't because I would be sneezing nonstop." Nick laughed, then abruptly quieted.

"When did your mom die?" he whispered.

"December 12, 1996," Joey answered back softly. This was the first time she had shared such a personal fact in passing. It felt sad, yet natural.

"Is that what you're upset about?" Nick asked. Joey looked up at Nick and smiled. If he could handle her talking about her mother dying and wedding plans . . . he certainly could handle a little haunting.

"No," Joey answered. "You see, really strange things have been going on all around me." Joey explained to Nick about the whispering, about the "X," and about the little girl she thought was Mary. "I know it sounds ridiculous, but it's really happening and I can't figure out why."

"You know what you need?" Nick said, comfortingly.

"A frontal lobotomy?" Joey offered.

"No," Nick laughed. "To relax."

Within twenty minutes Nick had Joey out in the ocean, sailing close to the reef. With hardly a ripple in the water, she felt silly in her fluorescent orange life jacket. But it was Nick's sailboat, and if he insisted she look like a ripe Sunkist orange, fine. Late afternoon was Joey's favorite time of the day. When the sky was a silvery pearl and the golden rays of sunlight beamed down through the clouds, it was heavenly. Joey settled into her seat, feeling more comfortable in her life jacket and surroundings.

Joey listened intently as Nick talked to her about his research and passion for his project. He told Joey about the first time he had ever seen the ocean—when he was sixteen years old. Until that age he had never been out of Colorado. His family went to visit relatives in Carmel, California and that's where he first saw the Pacific Ocean. He fell in love with the cliffs, the waves, and the marine life. Since then he had traveled not only to the Atlantic Ocean and the Gulf of Mexico, but to the Black Sea, the Indian Ocean, and even the Dead Sea. But in the last year, Nick had spent all of his free time—weekends, holidays, and vacations—traveling along the Eastern Seaboard, forming thesis ideas and gathering preliminary research. Ye after all his travels, it was a sea legend told by an old man in a tavern in Portsmouth that intrigued him the most. That legend, the Lighthouse Legend, was the first of many legends he wanted to prove true. Nick was convinced he knew exactly where the ship was and Joey admired his confidence and drive. Nick suddenly stopped talking.

Joey looked at him nervously, "What?" she asked, shyly.

"Manor Light is lucky to have you," Nick said sincerely. Joey blushed.

"How's that?" she questioned, not believing it. Nick pulled the tiller, turning the boat into shore.

"You're bringing it beauty." Nick pointed out the view of the lighthouse to Joey. From out in the water, it held a different look. The cliff didn't look as high; the powerful landmark seemed more cheerful, more alive. Joey smiled. This guy was great.

After helping Nick tie the sailboat to the dock, she took off her life jacket and hopped off the boat. Nick followed. He looked down at his feet, nervously. "I wanted to know . . . um . . . um . . ." He was having trouble getting the words out. Joey couldn't believe it. Was he really going to ask her out? She was excited. Not that she wanted to hurt Dawson, but he had acted like such a jerk about the whole thing. It wasn't like Dawson to be so blatantly dumb-guyish. Nick continued. ". . . um . . . would you be interested in learning how to dive? With me?"

Wait a minute, thought Joey. This wasn't the date she had anticipated. Nick continued. "I'm going on an initial dive at the end of the week and Dawson isn't exactly wet-suit friendly," he explained.

"Wet-suit friendly?" Joey questioned, disappointed.

"Dawson doesn't want anything to do with wet suits, breathing underwater, or flippers. But he did offer to film the entire recovery."

"So basically," Joey said, "what you need is another set of hands."

Nick grabbed her hands sweetly. "Another set of exceptionally nice hands." He smiled. Joey looked into Nick's green eyes. She could see herself in them. The image was a little distorted but it was her. Nick was looking at her the same way Dawson had the first time he noticed her, after the Miss Windjammer Contest. Joey smiled. It was nice to be noticed by someone. And this time she wasn't all dressed up with her hair done and makeup meticulously placed. This time she was just Joey Potter, wearing her favorite old pair of cut-off jean shorts and a faded Ice-House T-shirt. It felt good. The lighthouse, the cliff, the creepiness . . . were all starting to disappear.

Later that night, Joey was at home sitting on her dock. It was dark, but a full moon lit up the sky. She had been sitting there for two hours, in her comfy oversized pajamas, eating a watermelon and spitting its seeds out into the creek. She held a small tape deck in her lap—playing her favorite song over and over again. About to head inside, Joey noticed a familiar rowboat approaching. When she looked closer at the awkward figure rowing toward her, it wasn't Dawson. It was Jen.

"Jen?" Joey stood up, catching an oar as the boat nearly collided with the dock. "Since when did you ditch the Gramsmobile for a rowboat?"

"Dawson's rowboat," Jen answered, unsteadily. "Is it possible to get seasick on a creek?"

Joey laughed as she helped Jen tie a line from the boat to the dock. She reached out her hand to Jen and Jen toppled onto the dock, relieved to be on dry land. Joey looked at her, curiously. "I see Dawson's still in the habit of renting his rowboat out."

"He wasn't using it," Jen replied. "As we speak, Dawson and Pacey are in his bedroom watching *Indian Summer*, much to Pacey's dismay."

"Adults returning to their childhood camp to relive their juvenile relationships," Joey remarked dryly. "I wonder why I wasn't invited?"

"Just because a relationship happens when you're young, doesn't make it juvenile," Jen added, thoughtfully. She and Joey sat in silence on the dock, looking up at the stars. Joey took a deep breath, as fireflies swirled around her. A fish jumped out of the water and plunked back down. The tiny splash broke the peaceful moment.

"Do you think in ten years this whole time will just be an afterthought?" Joey asked, cautiously.

"Do you mean will Dawson be an afterthought?" Jen questioned. Joey stared down at her feet. Her sandals were dirty from the beach. She shrugged.

"Is it possible for two people of the opposite sex to really just be friends?" Joey wondered.

"Is this about Nick?" Jen asked.

"How do you know about Nick?" Joey questioned, defensively.

"Dawson told us the whole story." Joey was clearly upset so Jen explained, "When you rode home in complete silence today, Pacey and I were curious. And besides, Dawson is not a very good liar. Pacey quizzed him after he dropped you off and he said you were sick. And when I asked him what was wrong he said 'Lyme disease.' "

Joey rolled her eyes.

"You'd think a creative guy like Dawson could have done better than Lyme disease," Joey muttered. She looked at Jen, suddenly understanding why she was there. "Did you come over here to defend Dawson's angry outburst today?" No, Jen and Pacey were concerned about Joey's mental health. While Dawson's jealousies were blinding him to their friend's odd behavior, they were really worried.

"Actually, I've yet to forgive Dawson for an angry outburst thrown my way," Jen said. " But . . . Joey, look, it's none of my business, but you can't fault Dawson for being upset about your obvious interest in Nick." Jen frowned. She had wanted to ask Joey about Mary and the haunting. But she had wanted Joey to bring it up first.

"Is it that obvious?" Joey wondered.

"When Nick walked you to the car this afternoon, I could see it a mile away," Jen answered. "Give Dawson a break. He's just jealous."

"It's not his jealousy that's bothering me," Joey explained. "I went to Dawson with a specific problem and he didn't really care to help me."

"What problem?" Jen asked, clueless.

Joey gave her a look that said "Hello?"

"Is this still the whole lighthouse thing?" Jen asked, hopeful.

"Jen, I'm not crazy. I saw Mary Breckinridge on the beach today," Joey said, letting it all out. Jen listened intently. After Joey finished telling her saga, Jen sat silent for a moment.

"Voices are one thing. But seeing a ghost? She must want something from you."

Joey turned to Jen, surprised. "You believe me?" Joey asked, relieved.

"Sure I do," Jen lied. "If you were going to dream up a ghost friend for yourself, you would have been more original and made one up of your own." Joey laughed. Jen did her best to hide her concern. She really didn't believe Joey was seeing a ghost. No, she thought Joey had conjured herself an imaginary friend.

What did Dawson do when you told him?" Jen asked, continuing.

"Dawson might as well have just locked me inside the lighthouse with her. He was more concerned with my interest in Nick."

"That's a guy for you," Jen lamented. She stood up to leave. She needed to row back across the Creek and have a very serious heart-to-heart with Pacey and Dawson about this. She was worried about Joey, and her slight annoyance toward Dawson and his bogus accusations weren't going to get in the way of that concern. Although Jen was still holding a bit of a grudge, she hoped he would offer her and Joey the apologies they deserved. Joey continued with their conversation.

"Nick's different," Joey said. "He tried to get me away from the lighthouse, to help me get my mind off it. He asked me to help him with his internship. He wants me to learn to dive."

"And will you?" Jen asked.

Joey looked out into the water and grinned. "Yeah, I think I will. If I'm being haunted or going crazy, I might as well have some fun."

5

Holding Water

The next morning Joey showed up at the aquarium ready to learn how to dive. The underwater greenhouse was shimmering and calm. Jen and Pacey were out collecting seashells at the beach. Kate was busy in the big pool with Abigail. And most of the other sea life seemed to be sleeping late.

Joey counted her footsteps over to the diving area—it was an old habit that brought her comfort. She'd been up all night worrying which bathing suit to wear, and still wasn't convinced of her final decision. One hundred and fifty-seven steps later, Joey was still nervous.

Joey dropped her backpack on an iron bench,

looked up and was surprised to see Dawson in the pool.

"Where's Nick?" she asked, hesitantly.

Dawson swam around like a pro, flipping onto his back, then back onto his stomach. "He went to get the equipment for our dive," he answered.

"Our dive?" Joey asked. She wasn't sure what this meant. "Have you had a sudden change of heart?"

"Well, I started thinking," Dawson said, "and I realized this whole thing could be an adventure worth filming. Not only do I not want to miss out, I don't want to do it without you."

"Really?" Joey asked suspiciously.

Dawson nodded his head earnestly. "No cinematic achievement would be worth having without your sarcastic quips and comments. And besides, if you're that creeped out about the lighthouse, I'd rather you be here, with me." Joey started to take off her socks and shoes.

"And what about Nick?" she asked, curiously.

"If he's interested in you," Dawson said, thoughtfully, "then all I can say is . . . he has damn good taste."

Joey laughed and gave Dawson a knowing look. "Did you practice that line, Dawson?" she asked.

Dawson took a breath and sank under the water. He popped back up, closer to Joey. "Okay, I admit it . . . Jen told me to say that. But it worked, right?"

Joey nodded. "Yeah, it worked." It was a nice moment between Joey and Dawson. She couldn't stay mad at him too long. Besides, she didn't have time. Kate had agreed for her to have the morning off from her lighthouse duties. But, that was all. Joey had five hours to convince Nick of her scuba abilities, and for someone who doesn't scuba . . . that wasn't much time.

Joey took off her shorts and shirt, eager to begin. Instead of her usual two piece blue swimsuit, she wore a one-piece emerald tank dotted with pink flowers. Dawson looked at Joey's suit and laughed, "Uh, Joe, I think the Miss America Pageant is being held in Kansas this year. . . ."

Joey glared. "Do you see me in heels, Dawson? I don't think so. And F.Y.I.—the pageant no longer awards crowns for a well-fitted one-piece."

"No more bathing suit competition? So that's why Pacey didn't want to watch it this year," Dawson figured.

Meanwhile, Joey's insecurities were mounting. Although irritated by Dawson's remark, she needed to know. . . .

"Seriously, Dawson. Is it too much, too flashy, too . . . green?" Joey worried, looking at her swimsuit. Dawson knew who Joey was trying to impress. He didn't like her sporting a special swimsuit for Nick, but he was a man of his word, and chose not to give her a hard time.

"It looks great, Joey. You should wear it more often. You'll even show up the mermaids," Dawson said, climbing out of the pool.

"Thanks, Dawson." Joey smiled, more confident

now. She handed Dawson a towel and stepped down the first rung into the pool. The water was freezing. "Don't they have a heater we can turn on, or something?" she complained.

The door burst open and in came Nick, wheeling a cart with all the necessary supplies—wet suits, tanks, fins, masks. "Sorry, Joey, but the water temperature in the divers' pool is set for the ocean climate," Nick explained, stopping short in his tracks. With her dark hair and sea colored suit, Joey looked radiant.

Joey beamed inside, aware of Nick's admiration. Exuding confidence, Joey took another step down into the pool. Goose bumps quickly prickled her skin from the icy water. "It's not that bad," Joey fibbed.

Nick pulled three wet suits from out of his cart. "These should help make it a little more tolerable," Nick winked.

Dawson frowned. It had been one minute, and he was already tired of watching Nick and Joey's "first date" flirtation. He walked over and grabbed a wet suit off the cart. "Great. Then let the scuba lesson begin," Dawson said, reminding them he was still in the room.

Nick slipped on his wet suit, and jumped into the pool. He was just as anxious for Dawson and Joey to learn how to dive. After meticulously compiling bits and pieces of information from his studies, he felt he had the exact coordinates of the sunken ship. And with a salvage scheduled for the end of the week, six eyes searching were bound to be better than just two.

Practicing in the pool, Joey and Dawson got used to the tanks strapped to their backs. Joey was comfortable in her wet suit, but Dawson's was a bit small. Nevertheless, he was trying to be a good sport and not complain. Nick was positive he had located the ship; Dawson, however, wasn't so sure. But the fact remained, Joey was excited for the first time all summer and Dawson had almost ruined it once, so he was going to do his best not to ruin it again. If that meant squeezing into a wet suit two sizes too small and diving ten thousand leagues under the sea . . . fine. For Joey, he would. Even if she didn't know it.

An hour and a half later, Joey and Dawson were on their way to becoming "expert" divers. Well, at least expert beginners. Confident in their equipment and abilities in the water, Nick had led them out of the pool and down to the ocean. They were at a beautiful cove with rocks jutting out on either side. With the Institute, aquarium, and the lighthouse hidden behind them, Joey pretended she was on a far-off island.

With Nick in the lead, Dawson and Joey waded out until they were about thirty feet from shore. At the spot where the ocean floor quickly dropped from shallow to deep, they were ready to dive.

Nick explained that in scuba diving, divers had to speak to each other under the water with hand gestures. He showed them a few simple hand movements. Dawson laughed to himself; he had a "gesture" he'd like to give to Nick. As if reading his mind, Joey shot Dawson a disapproving look.

Joey pulled her mask down and put the oxygen tube into her mouth. She gave Nick a "thumbs up."

"Perfect," Nick said, as he pulled his own mask down. Dawson followed suit. With all of them having signaled "ready," they dropped down into the water.

They sank, letting the pressure in their ears equalize. Dawson seemed to be fine but Joey looked uncomfortable. The same sensation of loneliness that had filled her soul on the beach had returned. She couldn't shake it. And the added burden of this heavy, dark, deep, despair was pulling her quickly down into the sea.

Joey thought about little Mary Breckinridge. She was so young and died so cruelly. She thought about her own mother and the breast cancer that had taken her too soon. How Joey longed to see and touch her mother again. She'd tell her mother that she was okay, that she was a survivor. Then she'd hug her and tell her how much she missed her, begging her not to leave. But only in her prayers and her dreams were Joey's wishes ever granted. "Play with me Jo-sephine . . . play with me . . ." Mary's voice beckoned from the depths below her. "If you want to find answers, you'll find them with me. . . ."

Trying to shake the voice from out of her head, Joey's mask became filled with water. It covered her nose and rose to her cheekbones. She frantically gestured for Dawson and Nick to go up. The water filled her mask, covering her eyes. She couldn't see. She desperately clawed her way to the top, fighting against the strong force pulling her down.

At the surface, Nick popped up beside Joey. Dawson was already there.

"Are you okay, Joe?" Dawson asked with concern. Joey was breathing hard, scared.

"I don't know," she said, upset. "My mask filled up and my head felt like it was gonna explode . . ."

Nick was calm. "Don't worry about that," he said. "You just need to go down a little slower."

Joey nodded that she understood, deciding not to share what had spooked her. "And as far as your mask," Nick reminded, "remember what we practiced in the pool." He showed Joey how she could empty water out of it, even under water, by just pressing the top of the mask into her head and slightly lifting the bottom part. Joey remembered and was embarrassed. Dawson knew he could make her feel better.

"We've gotta go back down, Joe," he said encouragingly. Dawson held up his wrist. Attached to it was a disposable underwater camera. "We've gotta make this a Kodak moment." Joey laughed. Typical Dawson, capture every minute of his life, and hers, on film.

"Okay," Joey said, with growing confidence. "I'm ready." She pulled her mask down and put her tube back into her mouth. She was not going to let little

Mary Breckinridge ruin her fun. Who did she think Joey Potter was? She would show Mary . . . Josephine Potter was no wimp!

A cloud shifted and sunshine spilled out over the water. Joey smiled at the good sign. Together the three of them went down again. This time, Joey felt more in control. She got the hang of the breathing and of emptying her mask. It wasn't so difficult.

Once Joey's nervousness subsided, amazement and awe took over. She had never been this far under the water. Later, Nick estimated they were between fifteen and twenty feet down, but Joey felt like it was much more than that. All around her was a life she had never thought about before. There were schools of fish swimming by her. She saw coral and starfish. Dawson even pointed out a huge sea turtle. The plants looked like drawings in a storybook her mother used to read to her, the same book she now read to her nephew, Alexander, each night. Joey swam around, immersed in the new underwater world.

Dawson caught her attention and started snapping pictures of her. Having fun, Joey waved at the camera and spun around. Twisting and turning with her flippers and long floating hair, Joey was the image of a beautiful mermaid. Joey mugged for the camera for a few more poses, then reached out and took the camera from Dawson. It was her turn to take pictures of him.

Dawson took full advantage. He swam ahead of her, doing his best to ham it up for the camera. In full scuba gear, he pretended to reenact a scene from *E.T.*—where Elliot rides his bicycle into the sky. Joey loved it, because it described exactly how she was feeling at the moment. Weightless, soaring, and free.

Eventually, the practice dive had to end. Nick gestured to them and Joey and Dawson headed up to the surface.

Breaking through the water into the sunlight, Joey spit out her tube, ecstatic. "That was awesome!" she said, happily. "Nick, thank you so much. I can't even . . . I mean . . . Wow! I've never seen anything like that."

Dawson was pretty amazed, too. "Yeah, man. That was cool."

Nick was pleased. "So you guys think you're ready to help me find more than sand dollars and starfish?"

"Definitely." Joey smiled. "We're ready to help you find a sunken ship." Dawson smiled too, but inside, he was ill-at-ease. He was worried about Joey's stability, and he wasn't sold on Nick's designated coordinates for the Breckinridge ship. Nick might have just taught them how to dive, but he doubted Nick knew the correct part of the ocean to take them to search. Dawson had found no historical evidence pointing them to the right spot. To find the ship and the cause of Joey's trouble, Dawson knew they would need a better map—a better "X". For all of them, it was back to work as usual.

Tucking her polo shirt into her shorts, Joey scurried up the cliff path to the lighthouse. She was five minutes late for her midafternoon tour. When she reached the top, eighteen people were waiting impatiently by the locked door. "Figures it would be my largest crowd so far," Joey mumbled under her breath. A quick apology behind a cheery smile, and she had the ladies from Willowdale Retirement Village ready to bake her a pie.

Joey always led her tour groups to the top of Manor Light before telling them its history. She believed the ten-minute climb, soaking in the environment, made people eager for facts. However, because of the ages of the retirees, it took twice as long to get to the top.

Finally, they all reached the watchtower, the small room at the top of the lighthouse. Unlike the rest of the Manor Light, the room was bright, airy, and inviting. The observatory walls were constructed of tall glass windowpanes held together by bronze strips. A white wooden window seat circled the entire edge of the room.

Tired from their climb, the eighteen Willowdale women squeezed onto the wrap-around seat. Looking down at the landscape, they were amazed at the height at which they were seated. Joey walked to the center of the room and began giving them her tour.

"Lighthouses are fixed points that help sailors to navigate safely and find their positions," she explained. She continued, telling the ladies about

Manor Light's history, architecture, and beacon. "Because Cape Cod is prone to heavy fog, a light-ship with a sound guidepost was built farther into the sea thirty years ago. With the new and improved tower, Manor Light was no longer used," Joey said, concluding her speech.

Descending the spiral staircase to the bottom of the lighthouse always felt good to Joey. It was a reminder that her tour was almost over and she would soon be out in the fresh air.

Halfway down the staircase, Joey would stop at the only window built into the lighthouse's stone walls. Rectangular in shape and the size of a door, the window was rather plain. Its only adornment was a large crow's nest tucked into the corner ledge.

Every day Joey would drop the crows a few breadcrumbs from her lunch sandwich. She'd push the window out and extend her treats toward the nest. But like Abigail, the big black birds didn't seem to take to her. They would caw loudly and fly off over the ocean, circling until Joey was long gone from the lighthouse.

Back on the first floor, Joey would always nod to an old compass on the wall that pointed northeast. The circular instrument was framed in gold. It was no longer working but it had been there since the light-house was built. Ending her tour, Joey mentioned the compass to her group. "And to this day the compass is stuck pointing northeast," she stated.

"Doesn't look it to me!" piped up one woman.

"Honey, put your glasses on," responded another woman to Joey. The group burst into giggles. Joey glanced at the compass. She froze. It pointed in a different direction—Southeast. Somehow, despite being broken and unmovable, it had moved.

Joey stared at the compass, wondering if Dawson—or more likely, Pacey—was playing some sort of trick on her. No, she thought, they wouldn't be that cruel. Joey was positive the compass had been pointing northeast just hours before. Every tour, it pointed northeast.

Unlocking the glass case with her key, Joey tried to move the needle herself, but the hand wouldn't budge. Somehow Joey managed to a say a few final words, but all she could think about was the compass. Who could have moved it?

Kate leaned forward. "Congratulations. I hear you and Dawson had a successful dive with Nick this morning."

Joey shifted in her seat. "Yes, it was fun," she said, slouching down into her chair. Hesitantly, she looked around Kate's office.

Sensing some concern, Kate asked, "What is it Joey?"

"Well, I actually had a question about something else." Joey offered.

Kate smiled. "Sure, anything."

"Well," Joey said, "the compass in the light-house? I was under the impression that it didn't work."

Kate nodded. "That's correct. It hasn't worked in over a hundred years. It's stuck pointing northeast. It's just there for authenticity."

"Right . . . well, it moved. Today it was pointing southeast," Joey explained.

Kate shook her head. "That's not possible. It hasn't been functional since Woodland Beach was founded."

"But my tour group saw it. They even commented on it," Joey continued.

"The Willowdale Retirement Ladies?" Kate questioned, suspicious. She offered a suggestion. "Maybe everyone just misread it. You know, the late afternoon light can play tricks with the eyes."

"A broken compass doesn't just move on its own," Joey said, adamant. "I opened the case and tried to move it myself. It wouldn't budge."

Kate stood up, obviously not interested in the drama. "I'll check it out tomorrow, Joey. Don't worry. I'm sure it was a mistake and not a mystery."

Joey stood up and dropped the conversation. But she needed one final look at the compass before she would so easily laugh off her fears.

Borrowing Dawson's mountain bike, Joey raced back out to the lighthouse. Her late afternoon tour was about to begin, and once again she was running late. Joey hated being irresponsible. She parked her bike at the bottom of the cliff, and climbed her way up to the top. Rushing toward the lighthouse, she was surprised to see that no one was waiting.

Joey looked at her watch—she was five minutes late. The Oceano tour bus should have dropped off her group by now. Curious, Joey glanced up at the storm clouds rolling in overhead, and she found her answer. So worried about the compass, she had forgotten to walkie-talkie in for the status of her tour. And of course, due to bad weather, it had been canceled.

Joey kicked at the sand, angry at herself for being so absent-minded. She sat down on the bench and opened up her backpack. Having drunk all of her water, she settled for a Lifesaver. Sucking the cherry flavored candy between her teeth, Joey looked over at the empty lighthouse. Her desire to go inside and check the compass was increasing. Southeast? Northeast? Which would it read? But Joey had counted on looking at the compass while surrounded by a group of comforting strangers. Safety in numbers, she'd thought.

With the bad weather increasing, the wind swirled sand around the base of the lighthouse. Joey stared at the door. She was indifferent to the light rain beginning to shower her.

Twenty minutes later, her hair and clothes soaked, Joey ignored her gut feeling and walked over to the lighthouse. The door lock clicked open by itself as she was pulling out her key. Or had she left it unlocked in her rush to leave the earlier tour? Joey wondered. She pushed the door open and peered inside. "Mary . . . ?" she questioned, half joking to herself. No answer. Joey walked inside.

Standing on the first floor of the dark lighthouse, Joey strained her neck, and peered up into the watchtower. Through the glass she could see the dark, heavy clouds that had gathered overhead. The same feeling she'd had earlier on the beach and, again, in the ocean, swept over her. It was a feeling of dread.

Joey's mind shifted to another feeling of dread— her relationship with her father. She remembered the awful day Dawson told her that her dad was dealing drugs again. She remembered crying, not wanting to be the one to turn her father in to the police; sometimes what is right feels so wrong.

Joey gazed at the compass. She remembered arguing with Dawson after she'd helped the police arrest her father. "I understand that in the black-and-white world you live in, you don't see the choices," she had angrily yelled at him. "But that's not my world, Dawson. I see the gray."

And in Joey's gray world, she still wondered every day if she had made the right choice. She worried if her father would ever forgive her. It was an unanswered question that filled her with dread.

"Play with me Jo-sephine . . . play with me. . . ." Mary's childish voice called to her from the compass. "If you want to find answers, you'll find them with me. . . ." she charmed.

Joey slowly walked over to the compass. She really did see the gray in the world and right now she desperately wished someone else could see it, too.

Her feet tingling, her hands shaking, her mind believing in something unbelievable—Joey's eyes gazed upon the compass. Northeast. It was pointing northeast. Joey stared in disbelief. She was certain the compass had been pointing southeast earlier. It wasn't her imagination playing tricks on her. It had to have been real.

Suddenly, a streak of lightning cracked across the sky and thunder crashed around her. Joey scanned the room nervously. Her eyes stopped once again on the compass. But this time, the needle was racing around like a mouse in a cage. Mary's laughter swirled around with it and then rose up through the air to the top of the tower. "Play . . . with . . . me!"

Joey stared up into the watchtower. A rage in her swelled. Why was this happening to her? Why was this little girl being so mean to her? Joey didn't want to play with her. She wanted to be left alone. She wanted this haunting to stop.

Joey yanked the compass off the wall and raced outside. The metal needle, driven by a life of its own, continued to swirl—radically, wildly, around and around. Joey gripped the compass tightly in her hands as if it had been the source of every childhood pain.

Rushing to the cliff's edge, she held the compass out over the water. Angry at her mother for leaving her, angry at her father for betraying her, angry at herself for caring so much, Joey threw the compass out into the sea. She watched in silence as it tumbled to its death, driving deep into the stormy waters. Her anger was gone, but the dread still remained.

Joey walked back over to the lighthouse. Her head hung low, she was exhausted—both physically and mentally. She wanted nothing more than to go home, crawl into her warm bed, pull the covers over her head, and go to sleep. Maybe she'd pretend she was sick, and Bessie would make her tomato soup and little grilled cheese sandwiches. That's what big sisters were supposed to do. That's what her mother would have done.

Joey stepped up on the lighthouse landing to close the door. Her mind raced back to reality. What was she going to say to Kate? How much money was it going to cost to replace a hundred-year-old compass? Bessie would be so mad. Who was she kidding? There would be no little grilled cheese sandwiches or warm sheets. No. Bessie would want her to empty her piggy bank. Dawson, Pacey, and Jen already thought she was nuts. And Nick would never take her diving again.

Pulling shut the door to the lighthouse, Joey saw an image inside that was so real, so horrifying, her heart leaped in her body and her nerve endings froze. The compass was back, and perfectly positioned in its spot on the wall, the Atlantic's stormy seawater dripping down the metal and glass.

* * *

Dawson stood in the aquarium staring out the glass walls, watching the storm. He was worried about Joey. It was freezing, wet, and getting late. He knew her afternoon lighthouse tour had been canceled, yet Pacey had seen her headed up there on his bike. Joey hated Manor Light. It didn't make sense for her to go up there alone in the storm.

"Grand theft scooter. That's what you charge Potter with," Pacey exclaimed to Dawson. Pacey, standing by the pool, was hanging streamers for Abigail's baby shower. Pacey had initially made the suggestion to Jen as a joke. But Jen ran with the idea, thinking Abigail, her dolphin sensitivity similar to a human's, would be perked up by the party. Kate loved the idea, believing an improvement in Abigail's mental health would also boost her immune system. So, Pacey signed on as head party planner in hopes of impressing Kate. The crack of a thunderbolt snapped Pacey's attention back to Joey.

"I'll call Dougie and have him write Potter up a ticket," Pacey continued.

Dawson frowned. "I don't care that Joey took my bike without asking, Pacey. I'm worried about her being up there on that cliff all alone. And don't think I don't see you checking your watch every five minutes—you're worried too."

Jen was busy blowing up balloons, and tying them into big fun bouquets. "We all are. So why don't you two be the good heroes and trek on up there and save her," Jen urged. Dawson glanced at his watch.

"If Joey's not here in five minutes, we will," Dawson exclaimed.

Pacey was busy shaking his head "no" at the idea of going anywhere near the lighthouse. "Absolutely not. Take Jen. Whatever Joey's got . . . I'm not catching it!"

"It's called a wild imagination," Dawson explained. "We all know there are no such thing as ghosts. There are logical explanations for every disturbance that Joey's been experiencing."

"And how is that?" Jen questioned, skeptical. She knew Joey was heading off the deep end, and it bothered her that neither Dawson nor Pacey would face the real reason as to why.

"Simple. Subterranean caves. They're under all the buildings of Woodland Beach," Dawson answered.

Pacey wasn't buying it. "No, Dawson. You're wrong. The energy and echoes are coming from within Joey. Take a good look at her. She's living in the midst of someone else's life. And if Joey says it's 'Bloody Mary' Breckinridge, then who are we to disagree?"

"Please!" Jen scoffed.

"Joey is sensitive to the subject of death. Experiencing death makes you attuned to it," Pacey explained.

Cave energy, echoes, and a healthy imagination, that's the only thing Joey's attuned to," Dawson insisted.

Jen was getting frustrated. Pacey's streamers were

hanging too low, and her cheeks were tired from blowing balloons. "Give it up. You're both wrong. Joey's been wound up so tight her whole life, she's finally exploded. And now she's riding Dawson's bike somewhere over the cuckoo's nest. Bye-bye, see ya, hasta la vista, baby." Jen lost the balloon she was holding and it went flying through the room, letting out its air.

"Instead of worrying about ghostly creatures and subterranean caves, we should be trying to get Joey some seriously good mental health," Jen said, honestly concerned.

Dawson looked at his watch and gathered his things to leave. "Fine. Then let's go climb that cliff and bring her home," he urged. As Pacey began forming his excuses as to why he would not make a good candidate for the excursion, Joey walked into the aquarium. She looked at her friends numbly, then stared down deep into the pool. Abigail, like always, swam away from her. Dawson, Pacey and Jen watched Joey, not liking her abnormal silence.

"Where have you been?" Dawson asked tentatively.

"More importantly—what have you done with Dawson's bike and the real Josephine Potter?" Pacey teased, trying to lighten the moment.

Joey's eyes were puffy and red from crying. Soaked from head to toe, she looked like a drowning, helpless puppy. Her silence was not a calm one, but rather a paralyzed state of fear.

Joey glanced from Dawson to Pacey to Jen. She

was struggling to find the words, to ask for help. 'You guys don't know what it's like. . . . I just feel like I'm in this whole separate world from you, completely and totally alone. And no one can understand what I'm going through . . ."

"Everyone has loneliness, Joey," Jen said. She led Joey over to the pool to sit down. "The night Abby died, I saw a glimmer of her true soul. For the first time, she allowed me to break the surface and see something inside of her that was real and true— loneliness. You know, I still find it hard to think about the night she died. I wanted to save Abby when she fell off the dock. I wanted to save that lonely part of Abby Morgan that could understand my own loneliness. I wanted to save my friend, so she could in turn save me. But I let her down. Abby died that night. And I've been lonely a lot, before then and since then."

Dawson and Pacey stood in silence, respecting Jen's personal admission. Joey was taking in her every word. Jen continued, "Being there for a dolphin named Abigail doesn't make up for my not being there for Abby." Jen gestured to the party around them. "But it helps a little." She placed her arm around Joey's shoulder. "Being there for you helps us, too. We aren't going to let anything happen to you, Joey."

Joey reached down to pet Abigail, but Abigail flipped over and swam away. "I wish she would like me more," Joey said sadly.

"It took her a while to warm up to me, too," Jen

commiserated. "Forming a friendship with a dolphin is like—it's like trying to hold water in your hand."

Curious, Joey reached down and cupped her hands in the pool. She lifted a handful of water into the air. Slowly, it all leaked out.

Jen smiled, her theory proven correct. "You can't force it. It has to come naturally." Joey smiled. She liked the metaphor.

Joey reached her hands into the water again and cupped another handful. The water stayed in her hands a little longer, before it slipped through and dripped back into the pool.

Thirty minutes later, Joey was actually having a good time. Jen convinced her to forget about the lighthouse, at least for a little while. Joey, Dawson, Jen and Pacey were in the midst of celebrating Abigail's pregnancy—party favors, paper hats and all. Joey was serving her friends yellow cake and chocolate ice cream. Meanwhile, Jen was sitting on the edge of the pool helping Abigail open her gifts. She was keeping a little distance from Dawson. She was still a bit annoyed at his accusatory outburst from the other day. And Pacey and Dawson were playing pin the tail on the turtle.

Pacey kept missing the tail, aiming for the turtle's head instead. "This should count," he complained. "Heads, tails, they both tuck under the shell." Joey smiled as she brought them each a piece of cake. She and Dawson laughed at the paper turtle hanging on the wall. Pacey had hit every inch of its body but the tail. Pacey took his blindfold off, tired of the game. "I quit," he announced.

Joey walked over and brought Jen a piece of cake. Sitting down an appropriate distance away so as not to frighten Abigail, she smiled at all of Abigail's presents—a basketball, inner tube, and rather large baby bottle. Jen was stroking Abigail's stomach. Joey laughed, tickled.

"What?" Jen asked, curious.

"I didn't know dolphins had belly buttons," she smiled.

"Do they?" Dawson exclaimed, also surprised. He walked over and sat down at the edge of the pool with his cake to join them.

"Sure," Jen explained. "Dolphins might look like fish, but they're mammals. They have hair, breathe air, and have belly buttons just like you and me."

"They also mate and have sex, just like you and me," Pacey added, walking over. "And those Dolphin women, unlike Capeside women, are quite promiscuous." Everyone laughed.

Pacey sat down beside his friends. Crossing his legs, he rested his plate in his lap, and took a big bite of his cake. "I bet Kate has a cute belly button," he asserted, his mouth full.

The baby shower was winding down when Kate and Nick walked into the aquarium. Kate looked around at the decorations. "Wow!" she said, impressed. "This is incredible—even nicer than the last human baby shower I attended." She noticed the cake and melting ice cream. "You guys sure have gone above and beyond the call of duty."

"It was nothing," Pacey said, feigning modesty.

"Blowing up . . ." Kate looked around, counting all the balloons, "about twenty balloons? That's not nothing, Pacey. That's dedication." He smiled, in awe of her beauty and adoring the attention.

"I've got strong lungs," he replied. "I work out, ya know." Kate smiled. Jen rolled her eyes, knowing better. Pacey's lungs had practically deflated from blowing up one balloon. He had blown up the rest of the balloons using the oxygen out of the scuba tank.

Jen glanced down at Abigail, who had happily swam up to her. The baby shower seemed to be working. Abigail seemed more relaxed. Dawson walked over to join her by the side of the pool. He wasn't very happy. As soon as Nick had walked into the room, he and Joey had struck up a conversation, leaving Dawson feeling like the familiar third wheel. Pacey was engrossed in a conversation with Kate so Dawson sat down beside Jen, prepared to offer an overdue apology.

"You've been only slightly ignoring me the last couple of days. Does that mean you're less mad than you were?" Dawson asked tentatively.

"What makes you assume that?" Jen fired back.

"Well, you let me play Pin the Tail on the Turtle. . . ." Dawson reasoned.

"I put my feelings of hostility toward you aside

for Abigail's pregnancy and for Joey's sanity," Jen said. "But that doesn't mean you're forgiven." Dawson turned to face her.

"Jen, look," he began. "The other day I made a mistake. I was wrong to accuse you of trying to pull a prank on Joey. I know you wouldn't do that. I guess I'm just a little uptight—with all her sudden fears and now her interest in Nick. . . . I guess I just took out my frustrations on you. You're one of my very best friends and I hope you'll forgive me for being, basically, an unfeeling jerk." Jen smiled. Dawson sure knew how to articulate what was on his mind. She put her hand on his shoulder.

"Thanks, Dawson," she said, the sweetness back in her voice. "That means a lot to me."

Dawson smiled. "So . . . friends?"

Jen smiled back. "Friends."

"So, what do I do about Joey and Nick?" he questioned.

"Well, she was appreciative when Nick offered her an activity to get her mind off all the scary light-house—"

Dawson smiled. "Perfect, idea, Jen," he said. Dawson stood up and clapped his hands together, to get the room's attention. "Attention, everybody!" he said. "I have a proposition to make. Since we have all gorged ourselves on cake and ice cream, how about we work it off with a nighttime game?"

Pacey put his hands in the air. "No, no. No more 'turtle' for me."

"A new game, Pace," Dawson answered. "Reverting back to childhood games, why don't we play—"

Nick interrupted. "Flashlight tag!" Joey looked a little scared. And Dawson wasn't all that thrilled, either.

"No, Nick. I was going to say something like Marco Polo in the pool. And isn't it raining?"

"It stopped." Nick smiled. "Besides, who wants to run around and chase each other in the water when we can run around and chase each other in the dark?" Nick moved closer to Joey. "Don't worry, Joey. I'll protect you."

Dawson rolled his eyes. He glanced down at Jen and her bad advice. This wasn't exactly the outcome he had hoped for.

6

Playmates

The sky had cleared and although the ground was still damp, it was turning into a nice night to be outside. Concerned for Joey's mental health, being alone out in the woods and in the dark, Jen insisted the gang play Partner Flashlight Tag. Nick quickly paired with Joey. Pacey chose Kate. Which left Dawson and Jen rounding out team three. Within twenty minutes, a rousing game of Partner Flashlight Tag was in the works. The moon was full and it was a warm night. Kate, Pacey, Dawson, Jen, Nick, and Joey ran around the woods, behind the Institute, like eight-year-old kids. Regressing to childhood, their laughter rang out through the trees. It was a night of summer fun and good-natured competition.

Joey and Nick had already been "it" three times, as they scurried behind a large bush to hide. Joey kept peeking out from behind the leaves, to watch the light beam from the flashlight dance around the woods. Nick was busy, and happily content, staring at Joey. When a frog jumped on Joey's foot, Nick quickly came to the rescue by gently covering her scream with his hand. Joey looked up into his eyes appreciatively, and they shared a smile. With the moonlight pouring down around them, it was a fairy-tale moment.

But Joey didn't believe in happy endings, perfect moments, or perfect kisses. She remembered the time when Dawson took Jen up to the Ruins, trying to stage their first kiss—"the perfect kiss." She was so angry at Dawson. He kept practicing for weeks—kissing on a model's head he had used for one of his movies. And it was Joey the model looked like. How awful that had made her feel. She felt like the dummy head. She laughed so hard when the romantic moment Dawson had hoped for didn't work out. And it had really not worked out. He ended up capturing Pacey's R-rated "first time" with Tamara Jacobs instead of his own PG-rated "perfect kiss" with Jen.

Sensing a kiss, Joey looked up at Nick. He was the most attractive guy who had ever looked her way. Feeling his physical attraction, Joey stared into his eyes and saw a little deeper into his soul. He was complicated, but honest, she decided. Something was definitely going on inside him and inside her. She could feel the butterflies in her stomach.

Nick leaned in closer. Joey's heart began pounding so loudly, she felt as if everyone might hear. As Nick put his hand on the nape of her neck, the butterflies in Joey's stomach turned to giant Monarchs. Joey closed her eyes, both nervous and hopeful. She could feel Nick's lips coming dangerously close to hers, when suddenly a beam of light interrupted the moment.

Joey opened her eyes. Dawson was standing in front of them, the light from his flashlight splashing across Joey's stunned, reddening face. Dawson was stunned as well. Nick laughed and ran his fingers through his hair, slightly embarrassed, too. Jen stood beside Dawson, looking at Joey, amused.

"Having yourself a little *Summer of '42* of your own, Joey?" Jen teased.

Joey frowned at Jen's implication. "You're acting like I'm jail-bait, Lindley."

Jen shrugged. "Hmm. Seventeen candles on your birthday cake this year? Technically, you are."

Nick turned to Joey, aghast. "And you told me you were thirty-nine!" Joey and Jen giggled at Nick's one-liner. He was cute and clever. Witty quips were a must to run in this circle of friends. But Dawson wasn't interested in the show or Nick's quips. He handed over his flashlight, placing it into Joey's hand, hard.

"You're it," Dawson said, the anger evident in his voice. For a moment, Joey looked like a deer caught in the headlights, but, after a wide-eyed second, she burst out laughing.

"Again?" Joey said in disbelief.

Pacey shouted from a nearby tree, "Isn't there a statute of limitations on how many times you can wield the flashlight, Potter?"

Joey turned toward the tree. "Watch out, Witter! You're next." She counted slowly. "Five . . . four . . . three . . . two . . . one." When Joey turned around, everyone had disappeared, including Nick! She waved the flashlight around, looking for any sign of life.

"Hello . . ." Joey hollered into the woods. But nothing called back to her except the stillness of the trees.

Joey made her way over to a nearby patch of trees. She pointed the flashlight in its direction and saw a familiar face staring back at her—Nick! He pulled Joey into his arms and gave her a huge kiss. Just like that, with no preparation or planning. It was perfect.

"Excuse me?" Kate asked Pacey, offended.

Pacey and Kate were sitting behind a shed, underneath a worktable. Kate had been leaning in close to him. Pacey had been enduring their shoulders touching for ten minutes and was trying to summon up his courage to kiss her. He couldn't figure out why he was so nervous. He had handled rejection before. Actually, he felt he was getting pretty good at it. Compared to Dawson, he was practically a certified stud. So, he took a deep breath, went in for a kiss, and got shot down.

"I repeat. What do you think you were just trying to do?" Kate demanded to know.

"Should I have asked you out on a date first or something?" Pacey asked, clueless.

Kate crawled out from under the table, "No, no. That's not it."

Pacey followed behind her. "Because," he continued, "I'd love to do dinner, a movie, a walk on the beach . . ."

Kate frowned, "Pacey, no!"

"If you're worried about Dougie's homosexuality genes running in the family—don't worry, I was adopted!" he fibbed.

Her annoyance turned to pathetic sympathy. Kate laughed. "Look Pacey, I'm flattered. But I think I'm a little too old for you. I'm twenty-six. You've been driving what . . . a year?"

Pacey laughed. "Hey, I've been 'driving' for a very long time, if you know what I mean. I even dated a woman way older than you." Kate looked at him in disbelief.

"Pacey, you don't have to lie," Kate said.

Pacey snapped back, firmly. "Seriously, Kate. I can give you references. I'm mature for my age—"

"Then you should be able to understand rejection without me having to spell it out," Kate said, wanting to laugh.

Pacey raised his arms in denial, "I see. So, it's the inter-office relations no-no rule."

Kate nodded. "Yes, among other things . . ."

Pacey lowered his head, feeling a little sorry for himself. "Who would have thought one kiss would be so out of Pacey Witter's reach?" he muttered to himself. Kate sweetly reached down and picked up Pacey's hand. She pressed the palm of his hand to her lips.

"Keep trying," Kate said. "Not with me, of course. But keep trying. There's a natural beauty out there and she's waiting just for you." Pacey was touched, and wanted to kiss Kate on the lips even more. He watched her walk toward the Institute, having called it a night.

While it had been fun, Pacey's romantic gesture had made Kate feel a little juvenile, standing out in the woods playing Partner Flashlight Tag. Kate stopped halfway back to the Institute, and turned around to look at Pacey. Pacey tried to glance to the side, to act like he hadn't been watching her.

"Hey, Pacey," Kate hollered. Pacey turned around to her like he was just noticing her.

"Yeah?" he hollered back. He was hopeful. Maybe Kate had changed her mind.

"Have you ever thought about asking out Jen?" Pacey smiled.

Jen and Dawson were stationed inside the shed. With its dirt floor, and holes in the tin roof, Jen wasn't too happy with Dawson's choice for a hideout.

"I don't think coming in here was such a great idea, Dawson. I'm seeing lots of dirt and feeling lots of cobwebs," Jen said. Dawson took off his jacket and threw it on the ground for Jen to sit on.

"Here, quit your complaining," Dawson said, obviously upset.

Jen sat down on his coat. "Now that we've renewed our friendship," she said, "do you want to talk about it?"

Dawson shook his head. "What's the point?"

"Well, for one, if we resolve your jealousies about Nick being with Joey, it might get me out of this stink-pot faster." Jen glanced around. "I'm guessing snakes, mice and really big spiders—"

"Shhh, I'm weighing my options," Dawson said tersely. He sat down on his coat beside Jen. While not a fan of spiders or snakes, all Dawson could think about was Nick and Joey. Nick! Mr. Captain Ahab himself, out there behind some tree making a move on his soul mate. Dawson didn't like it. He wanted Joey back. He needed a plan.

"Accept the drama and move on," Jen advised. "Nick's a summer romance. That's all."

"You think?" Dawson asked.

"Yes," Jen assured. Dawson shook his head, letting the romantic scenario Jen offered sink in. Always jumping to the worst-case scenario when it came to Joey Potter and her love life, Dawson hadn't thought about that distinct possibility. He knew about summer flings. He'd had them himself. Yeah, he could probably deal with a summer fling.

"You think?" Dawson asked again.

"Yes," Jen assured. The two sat in silence for a

very long time. Dawson continued to worry about summer romances and Jen continued to worry about the spiders.

"I remember another time when we were ducking down, hiding like this," Jen teased.

Dawson nodded. He remembered, too. "The Ruins. I tried to stage the perfect kiss."

Jen sighed. "The perfect lighting, the perfect location, the perfect time of day . . ."

"Yeah," Dawson sighed, looking at Jen. He could remember why he had liked her so much. At the time, he even thought it was love. Now, here she was, beside him, while Joey was enthralled with Nick. Dawson wondered if he hadn't been so insecure about Jen's sexual past, if things could have been different between them. It was almost as if Jen could read his mind.

"Wait a minute, Dawson," Jen said, skeptically. "You have that look in your eye . . ."

"What look?" he asked, innocently.

"That I'm-contemplating-kissing-you-because-Joey-was-almost-lip-locked-with-some-grad-student look," she said, matter-of-factly.

Dawson laughed. "The thought did occur to me."

"Well, un-occur it, Dawson," Jen said. "Didn't we just establish what we are?"

Dawson nodded. "Friends."

Jen smiled, adding, "Besides, Dawson . . . that kiss at the Ruins? While mostly perfect, it still wasn't perfect in one way—"

"How?" Dawson asked.

"I wasn't the perfect girl," Jen answered. Dawson leaned in and gave his good friend a kiss on the cheek. Dawson knew why he liked Jen so much. She was able to call a spade a spade and accept it! If only he could do the same—maybe his teen angst would subside.

Joey and Nick were "it" again as they ran around looking for everyone. This had been the fifth time Joey had been "it," and it had been her fault every time. Nick was great at dodging the light. Joey might as well have had a huge bull's-eye on her forehead. But Joey didn't mind being "it" if it meant the game could go on forever. She loved running around like a kid, laughing, screaming, and sneaking a few kisses here and there with Nick. It was a fun kind of scared, not a lighthouse kind of scared.

Joey was having so much fun, she didn't argue when Nick suggested they split up and double their chances of catching someone. She reveled at the thought of finding Dawson and shining the bright light in his eyes. She snuck around the side of the shed and creaked open the door. Hearing a noise, she pointed the flashlight in the sound's direction. A familiar face stared back at her—but it wasn't Nick, Dawson, Jen, Pacey, or Kate. It was the face of Mary. A bloody Mary.

Joey let out a scream, but her voice was so shaken it sounded more like a gurgle. She ran outside into the woods. Tripping, she smacked against the base of a large tree. Pulling herself up, Joey panicked as the withering branches began twisting tightly around her body. She kicked them off wildly and frantically. Feeling the familiar sense of dread rising up high in her chest, Joey clawed her way up to her feet. She let out a blood curdling scream. Kate came running from the Institute but Nick was the first to reach her.

"Joey?" he called out. Joey was shaking, near tears. "Joey!" Nick grabbed her. "Are you okay?"

Joey shook her head. "I thought . . . I thought . . ."

Nick looked into her eyes. They were full of fear. "You thought what?" he asked, concerned.

"I saw Mary. I mean, I think I saw Mary. Whatever I saw, she was awful." Joey was getting frustrated trying to explain herself. "I can't put it into words, Nick. . . ." Joey's mind was racing in a midst of madness that no one else could understand. They could try, they could even believe her, but they couldn't see what she was seeing. Her eyes filled with tears. This couldn't keep happening again and again. Joey shook her head. "I can't go back there. I can't."

Nick placed his arm around Joey and steered her to the parking lot. "Don't worry, Joey, it'll be all right," he said, comfortingly. Nick turned to the group. "Don't worry guys, I'll take Joey home." Joey was surprised that no one argued, not even Dawson. She walked off with Nick to the car, feeling more alone than she had ever felt before.

Dawson, Pacey, Jen, and Kate looked at each other,

not completely understanding what had just happened.

"Is she okay?" Kate asked, worried.

"She just needs to get some sleep," Dawson said. But in his heart, Dawson was finally accepting that Joey needed a lot more than sleep.

The next morning was hot and sticky. Once again, the four were on their way to work. Dawson glanced in his rearview mirror at Joey. Instead of riding shotgun, she had climbed into the backseat. She hadn't said a word all morning. It was as if she were forcing Dawson to drive her to her own funeral.

"You don't have to go in, Joey . . . okay? We can turn around right now," Dawson said in a calming voice. He hadn't slept a wink all night, worrying about Joey. He wanted to stand up to Nick and drive Joey home last night, but, earlier in the evening she had made it pretty obvious with whom she wanted to spend her time. Dawson sighed. He had no solution for her problem—period.

Jen, sitting next to Joey in the backseat, was equally concerned. "Yeah, Joey," she added, "It's just an internship. No one will care if you miss a day." Jen had her own conclusions as to what Joey Potter's problem was. She needed a good psychiatrist. But she knew Joey, and Joey would never pour out her soul to a complete stranger, not even to Nick.

"No, you guys, let's go on. I'll be fine," Joey stated. She glanced at her friends, her brown eyes telling them how grateful she was for their concern. Dawson's attitude during flashlight tag had hurt her. What right did he have to be jealous of a kiss? And she had been even more hurt when he hadn't demanded to take her home. But what did she expect? Kiss one guy and go home with another? Joey looked out her window again, sulking, knowing she had no one to blame but herself.

Pacey watched Joey from his side-view mirror. He was happy to be riding shotgun, but not under someone else's duress. Typical Joey, blaming a haunting on herself, he thought. He could read her mind as sure as his own. The solution to Joey's problem seemed simple to Pacey. Joey should stay away from that creepy, spooky lighthouse. "Are you sure, Joe? You know, you don't have to do anything you don't want to do, Potter," Pacey piped in.

"I'm sure, Pacey. Don't worry. I'll be fine," she insisted. Joey continued to stare out the window, silently beating herself up in her mind. She was tired of running away from her fears. Sure, the sight of the returned compass sent chills down her spine, but it also had proven something to Joey: there *was* something happening that was out of her control. She knew that resisting it wasn't going to make it go away. Joey was too old to run from her problems and fears. She had faced her fears before—visiting her dad in prison, rallying people behind Principal Green, kissing Dawson, following her heart with Pacey. And now it was time to face them again—with a little girl named Mary Breckinridge, who wanted her to play.

"So, I'm debating my strategy for Kate," Pacey said, hoping to lighten the mood. "I'm thinking of playing hard to get." Jen and Dawson laughed.

"I'm sure she'll view that as a welcome relief, Pace," said Dawson matter-of-factly. Pacey leaned back in his seat, quiet. Jen eyed Joey, getting an idea.

"Pacey," Jen said, "I'm going to go out on a limb here and guess you have no big plans for the workday. . . ." Pacey looked at Jen suspiciously, wondering what exactly she was getting at.

The next thing Pacey knew, he was standing in the doorway of the lighthouse, surrounded by tourists, trying desperately to remember all of the information Joey had hurled at him in the car. While on a mission to be strong, Joey jumped at the chance for a break from the lighthouse. She rationalized it would give her time to form a game plan on how to deal with Mary's haunting.

"Did you know that local dolphins actually navigate these waters using the lighthouse as a checkpoint?" Pacey asked his incredulous crowd of tourists. Pacey grinned to himself. No one was going to forget his mighty special lighthouse tour!

Joey wiped her forehead and straightened her hair as she climbed the stairs to the Rare Books Room. The morning had been a scorcher. The ocean and beach had long lost the battle with the blazing sun and the torrid humidity had turned the aquarium into a steam bath. With Pacey giving tours at the lighthouse, Joey had planned to help Jen at the aquarium. But Abigail had become rather cranky overnight and was refusing to eat. With Joey only aggravating Abigial more, Dawson rose to the occasion and took over Pacey's fish tank duties. Which left Joey internship-free and in the air-conditioned Rare Books Room with Nick.

Joey entered the room and found Nick hard at work. "Hey, Joey," he said, barely looking up from his work. Was this the same guy she kissed last night during flashlight tag?

Joey shifted uncomfortably. "Hi."

Nick ran his fingers through his hair. He looked tired.

"What are you doing," she asked.

"I'm digging around for more wreckage information," Nick replied. "Do you mind giving me a minute? I just need to finish this up." Joey nodded. She felt embarrassed. Nick was treating her like an intruder.

Joey looked around for something to do. A large globe sat on a waist-high bookshelf. It was rotating—ever so slowly. Reminded of her episode with the compass, Joey was about to run from the room. Then, the air conditioner cut off and the globe slowed to a stop. Joey sighed in relief. It was only the force from the blowing air vent that had made the globe turn. She laughed off her fear and gave the globe a playful spin. Something caught her eye on the wall, just left of the globe. The pattern of the wallpaper seemed to form a series of numbers. She squinted her eyes to look at it.

"Nick, look," Joey said. "There are numbers here." Nick was so engrossed in his research, he seemed not to hear her. Annoyed, Joey dismissed the patterned wallpaper and headed for the door. Usually, when Joey was interested in someone—for instance, Dawson or Pacey—it was accompanied by months or even years of angst and stress. A summer crush was supposed to be simple and fun. If Nick was going to turn her crush into anything else, he'd have to do it alone. But before Joey could leave, Nick looked up.

"Joey, wait," he said, closing his book and standing up. "I have something to tell you."

After a long morning of internship switcheroo, Dawson, Pacey, and Jen joined Joey for lunch in the Taylor Museum. They sat, for the most part in silence, at a small corner table, surrounded by shelves of books, eating lunch in the cool air. Joey unrolled her lunch, quickly glancing around at everyone else's. Closest to the air-conditioning vent, Jen was enjoying the cold air blowing on the back of her neck and a food-free diet. Pacey, having forgotten his lunch, was sharing Dawson's submarine sandwich and thermos of chocolate milk. Joey looked down at her own lunch. Peanut butter and jelly sandwich, chips, and an apple—Bessie had packed the Potter version of a well-balanced lunch again.

Chomping on her apple, Joey shared Nick's news. He would be leaving later that afternoon for Boston. Having exhausted his resources in the Taylor Museum, he wanted to do some more research in another library before their scheduled dive at the end of the week. This was news to Dawson. It seemed Joey knew more about his own internship than he did. Although Nick would only be gone for a few days, the look of disappointment on Joey's face was evident. Dawson, however, was ecstatic. And Joey could tell. "Well, don't be too overjoyed," she snapped.

"What?" Dawson said, feigning ignorance. But inside, he was jumping for joy that Mr. Summer Romance was shoving off to sea. Dawson wanted to win Joey over, and now he had the opportunity to do so. As Dawson dug into his almost gone sandwich he formed his plan. . . .

Joey took another bite out of her apple. Gazing around the room, she imagined what would have happened if Nick had asked her to join him in Boston. Nick had an apartment in Cambridge that he sublet to a friend for the summer, but the friend certainly wouldn't have minded if Joey and Nick had crashed there for a couple of nights. They were on official business, after all. It could have been romantic—research by day, romance by night.

Joey imagined what nice places Nick would take her to for dinner. Maybe they would even have gone dancing. Not that Joey particularly loved dancing—her lessons with Pacey at the Starlight

Dance Studio proved she had two left feet. But this was her fantasy, after all, and in her fantasy, if Nick liked dancing, she liked dancing. In her fantasy they would salsa, boogie, and hustle. But, unfortunately, it was a fantasy—slow dancing with Nick under the Boston moonlight was pretend. Eating a melted PBJ, while worrying about an angry ghost . . . that was reality.

After lunch, Jen and Pacey returned to the aquarium to find Kate and a veterinarian standing at the pool's edge. Abigail was in labor, a month early. The dolphin was swimming around and around in circles.

"What's she doing?" Jen asked, concerned.

"It's okay, Jen," Kate answered. "This is normal behavior. Her calf will be born any moment now." Jen ran over to the edge of the pool, both excited and concerned. She watched, entranced, as Abigail entered into motherhood. Jen wanted to stroke the top of her back but was afraid to distract her. She didn't know childbirth etiquette, least of all with dolphins. She remembered when Joey's nephew was unexpectedly born during Hurricane Charles. Jen stood with Joey, while Grams delivered Alexander.

Pacey plopped down on a bench, queasy. "I don't know if I can watch this . . . I just ate."

"It's the miracle of childbirth, Pacey," Kate said. "Of course you can watch." Pacey thought about the chocolate milk he had just gulped down for lunch. He needed to put his "hard to get" plan into fast action—as in look *hard* for a way *to get* out of there! Pacey stood up to exit, when Jen began hollering frantically. . . .

"Oh, my gosh, the baby dolphin is coming out tailfirst. She's breaching, she's breaching!" Jen exclaimed. Pacey made his way over to a trashcan for fear of losing his lunch. Jen stood up and began pacing the pool. She was losing it. She couldn't stand to see anything happen to Abigail. Kate walked over to Jen and put her arm on her shoulder.

"Jen, it's okay. Dolphins are born the opposite of how human babies are. They come out tailfirst. Not headfirst."

"Really?" Jen asked, still a little worried.

"Really," Kate said, comforting. "Abigail's just fine." Jen let down her shoulders in a sigh of relief. She didn't like feeling helpless, and she was already feeling helpless about Joey. Calmer, Jen returned to sit at the pool's edge to wait for Abigail's baby dolphin to emerge. Within ten minutes, the baby had arrived. The vet examined the calf and made the announcement.

"Congratulations, Abigail," he said, "it's a girl!"

Jen smiled. "What should we name her?" Jen asked Kate.

Kate glanced at Jen, "I think it only appropriate if you do the honors."

Jen was pleased by the offer, but her anxiety had left her mind blank.

"I don't know," Jen said, stumped. Then, thinking back to her own self-imposed name . . . "What about Bubbles?"

Kate walked over to the side of the pool and rubbed Abigail's head. "Do you approve of the name?" With her smiling bottlenose, Abigail swam over and nodded her head "yes"!

The following day, against Jen's, Dawson's, and Pacey's wishes and advice, Joey resumed command of her Manor Light duties. She wasn't going to let her fears get the best of her. Her first tour had gone well, so she decided to reward herself during her lunch break. Joey gathered up her art supplies and took them out to the cliff. She wanted to sketch the ocean and the jetty just as the sun was at its highest point in the sky. She looked around, sketching intently and worked until she had the entire seascape outlined.

Joey took a break, stretching out her legs in the sun. She frowned at her farmer's tan. Suddenly, she heard a quiet voice behind her.

"Are you mad at me, Josephine?" Joey turned around and squinted into the sun. No one was there, but she could feel the familiar presence of the little girl. Joey set down her sketch pad.

"Mary? Is that you?" She heard the little girl's voice giggle around her ear. It sounded like she was twirling around, dancing with happiness.

"Are you ready to play with me, Josephine?" she asked. Joey gave in to Mary's request. She wanted all of this to end.

"Sure, I'll play with you. What do you want to play?" Joey answered.

"Dolls!" the voice demanded, ecstatic. Joey continued looking around for a person to put with the voice, but there was none.

"But I have no dolls to play with, Mary," Joey answered. She suggested another game. "Have you ever played 'favorites'?" Joey asked.

"What's 'favorites'? " the little girl asked.

"You know, favorite color, favorite toy, favorite movie—" Joey rattled off.

"Blue—because that's the color of heaven," Mary answered. "My doll—because my mother made it for me, and I do not know what a 'movie' is." Joey realized there was a time lapse of a couple of centuries between the two of them. She laughed to herself. What would Dawson think of someone who did not know what a "movie" was?

"Do you like to draw?" Joey asked her. She reached over to get her sketch pad and saw that her drawing had been mysteriously colored in. The right colors were used but they were not contained between the lines. It was as if a child had filled it in. An eight-year-old child named Mary. Finally, Joey had hard evidence. She stood up, excited to race down and show the drawing to her friends. She wanted to prove to them that she wasn't crazy.

However, quickly realizing the reality of the situation, she dropped to the ground, defeated. No one would believe her. They would think that Joey had done it. Finally giving into the dread, Joey began to cry. To sob. Hard tears. Tears she hadn't cried since her mother was dying. And as she did, Mary's hand reached hers and a voice said . . .

"Don't cry, Joey. I didn't mean to hurt your picture. I can erase it." Joey looked beside her. There, holding her hand, was the little girl she had seen on the beach pointing to the "X" carved in the tree. She was beautiful, radiant, like an angel. Joey squeezed Mary's hand back, tightly.

"Don't cry, Joey," Mary said. She wiped hair away from Joey's face. "We'll take care of each other. We can play together." Joey smiled. She could see Mary—this was real.

"So you do like to draw!" Joey said. "I guess that means you and I have something in common."

Mary replied, "We have quite a bit more than coloring in common, Josephine."

Joey nodded, knowingly. She was talking about being separated from her parents. "Yes," she said, "I think we do."

The rest of the day and all of the next, Joey was referred to by Dawson, Jen, and Pacey as M.I.A.—missing in action. Mary had woven herself a web, and Joey had flown right into it. She fell in love with Mary and her playful spirit. No longer scared, she felt free and alive, much as she had playing flashlight tag. Joey didn't worry about trying to prove Mary existed, she just wanted to be in her presence. Maybe Mary hadn't been haunting her—maybe she was just trying to get Joey's attention. Joey didn't want to be apart from her new friend.

They spent every spare moment Joey had, together, often painting in the watchtower at the lighthouse. Mary pointed out colors to Joey. Joey taught Mary how to sketch land and seascapes. They played hide-and-seek around the cliffs. Once, Joey came dangerously close to falling when a rock slipped out from beneath her foot. Mary protected her by pulling her away from the ledge. They took long naps under the big oak tree and Joey would pack a children's book every day and read it to Mary under the tree. They would stare out into the ocean together and make up fantastic stories of kings and queens in a world full of dragons, unicorns and fairies.

Joey was having exactly what she had wished for at the beginning of the summer. A mindless, fun-filled summer she could recapture her soul in. But Joey knew there had to be a reason why Mary had shown herself to her. She thought of the compass and the "X" carved into the tree. There had to be something Mary wanted besides a playmate.

"Mary," Joey asked cautiously, "were you in the Rare Books Room with me on the first day I came to the Institute?" Mary was quiet. "Have you seen the numbers on the wallpaper?" Mary's face indicated that she knew what Joey was referring to but she still said nothing. "Mary, what do those numbers mean? You know, don't you?"

Mary stood up. "I don't want to talk about this," she said, her voice suddenly serious and stern.

Joey looked at her, blankly. "Mary, what don't you want to talk about?" Joey thought for a moment. "Is it your parents?"

Mary shook her head and answered, "My parents left me. I don't want to talk about them."

"Mary, I understand how you feel," Joey said, sympathetically. "My parents also . . ."

"I don't want to talk about it!" Mary backed away, angry at Joey for bringing it up again. And slowly, Mary's image faded into nothingness.

7

Bittersweet Scent of Roses

Driving to work the next morning, Dawson and Joey were distracted. The last two days had brought an increasing distance and tension between them. With Nick away in Boston, Dawson had been hoping to spend quality time with Joey. Instead, Joey was spending a large amount of time at Manor Light. She had completely checked out of their friendship. Dawson was desperate to know why. She had gone from terrified to obsessed.

Joey sat beside Dawson, watching him ignore stop signs, yellow lights, and a variety of other traffic signals. She, who usually screamed the rules of the road from the front seat, was surprisingly quiet. Today, Joey was even more anxious to get to the

Institute than Dawson. Today was the day for their dive with Nick.

"Can't you go any faster?" Joey exclaimed, impatiently. She held a tight grip on the door handle, preparing for the moment Dawson parked the SUV. She wanted to be ready to jump out and run into the Taylor Museum. Dawson noticed Joey staring at the speedometer and lead-footed the gas.

Meanwhile, Jen and Pacey were holding on for dear life in the backseat. They clumsily put their seat belts on to prevent themselves from sliding across the slippery leather onto one another. Jen frowned as Pacey slammed into her side, his face coming dangerously close to hers. Dawson took a sharp turn around the bend. This time it was Jen who went flying across the seat into Pacey. Her hair and Aqua Net getting caught in his mouth, Pacey had had enough.

"Dawson!" Pacey finally yelled, exasperated. "Slow down, man. You want Dougie to come after us with his flashing blue and red lights?"

Dawson looked at the speedometer. It read 90 mph. He slammed on the brakes. "Sorry."

"We're going to work. To do free labor. For a total of eight hours, Dawson," Pacey said. "There's no rush."

"Actually," Joey said, turning around, "there is a rush. I want to make sure I find Nick first thing. I don't want him leaving for the dive without me."

"Me, too," Dawson said, smiling at Joey. But Dawson wasn't worried about seeing Nick. No, he was excited to have an excuse to spend some time with Joey. That was what Dawson was hoping for. A day out in the ocean on a small boat would be just fine. It was his chance to prove to Joey who was the better man.

Joey turned back around and looked out the window, conflicted. But not about Dawson. She had enjoyed the last two days spent without him. His jealousy had only burdened her more. Joey was worrying about Nick and Mary.

While excited that Nick was returning from his trip, Joey regretted having to pass off her lighthouse tours. The inner child in her felt good spending her days on the cliff—reverting back with Mary to days of fun and games. But the older, more mature Joey had missed Nick. And this older Joey was smiling inside—knowing that in just ten minutes she would get to see the current object of her affection. Nick!

Jen was ready for her own exciting day. Kate was going to let her in the water with Bubbles for the first time. She couldn't wait to lead the baby dolphin around the pool. Abigail was being protective of Bubbles, so Jen wanted to get to the aquarium as soon as possible to have plenty of reassurance time. Jen had been relieved that Abigail was all right, despite the premature arrival of Bubbles. Jen had been a premature baby and had had a difficult birth, too. Her own mother never let her hear the end of it—as if Jen had intentionally decided to interrupt her mother's bridge game!

"Actually, Pacey," Jen said out of the blue, "I'm in

a bit of a hurry to get to work as well."

Pacey laughed, as he slid his baseball cap low on his head. The bright morning sun was adding to his headache. "Whatever, Lindley," he cracked.

Dawson did a sharp turn into the parking lot and wheeled into a space. He hopped out of the car and tossed Pacey his car keys. "You're the man," he said sprinting off toward the museum. Grabbing her bag and slamming her door, Joey was right behind him.

Pacey caught the keys in his hands and looked at the shiny SUV in disbelief. "Commando of the Leery wheels? Did the Breckinridge ship go down in the Bermuda Triangle or something? You guys are planning to come back, aren't you?" he hollered after Joey and Dawson.

Almost at the door of the Institute, Joey turned around and made a mean face. "Okay, Pacey. That's not even funny," she hollered back, not amused.

Jen rushed off toward the aquarium to see Bubbles. "Good luck, you guys," she hollered to Joey and Dawson. As Jen slipped out of sight into the woods, Joey and Dawson entered the Institute.

All alone, and left with the keys, Pacey looked at the vehicle questioningly. He stood there, wasting a full two minutes, wondering if he should hop back in, drive back home, and take a long morning nap. His conscience getting the best of him, he decided to go into work—to flirt with Kate. As he always said, "Witters weren't quitters!"

* * *

Jen nervously prepared to climb into the pool

with Abigail and Bubbles. She sat down on the edge of the pool to watch the mother and child swim together and to contemplate her strategy. To her left, Pacey was getting acquainted with two new turtles that had been brought into the Institute early that morning. Kate was standing beside him, observing the turtles in one of the smaller pools.

"I can think of some names for them," Pacey offered, eager for attention.

"Sure, Pacey," Kate said, not really listening. "Whatever you want."

"So tell me about them," Pacey asked, desperate for some communication. Kate pointed to the largest turtle, gray and with a very long tail. It was about twenty inches long.

"This is a female snapper. We found her on land, nesting. Police had received some reports of aggressive behavior, so they brought her here," Kate explained. Pacey backed away from the vicious animal and walked over to the smaller, seemingly more friendly turtle. It was about five inches in size and looked more like a large algae-covered stone than a reptile.

"Tell me about this one," Pacey encouraged.

"He's a musk turtle. They're fun to watch. They can stretch their necks all the way to their back legs," Kate answered. Pacey reached out to touch the animal. . . .

"Pacey, don't!" Kate hollered. But it was too late.

Before Pacey had even reached his hand to pet it, the turtle released a very foul-smelling liquid.

Kate laughed as she and Pacey hurried away from the terrible odor. "The musk turtle is also known as the 'stinkpot!' " Kate advised.

"Now you tell me." Pacey rolled his eyes, feeling rather foolish. He wasn't going to win Kate over smelling or acting like this.

Kate walked over to the diving pool and began to undress, down to her bathing suit.

"I'm going to jump in and get rid of the smell," Kate said. Pacey watched Kate unbutton her blouse and climb out of her shorts. She wore a crystal blue one-piece bathing suit that exactly matched her eyes. She filled it out quite nicely. With her curves and long red hair, she looked like a siren. Kate sank into the water and waved to Pacey.

"Come on in, the water's great," Kate urged.

Pacey peeled off his clothes, down to his bright red swim trunks, and ran over to the water in ten seconds flat. He climbed into the pool. Trying to act cool, he smiled and said, "So glad you invited me!" His voice cracked like a boy going through puberty. Kate tried hard not to laugh at his unintentional "Peter Brady" impression. Arching her back, she kicked off the bottom of the pool and swam backward toward the deep end. Meanwhile, Jen had been watching Pacey's sad attempt at flirtation.

"Give it a break," she hollered over to Pacey. Pacey gave Jen a stern look that said, "Mind your own business." Jen walked over to the diver's pool just to annoy him. Joining them in the water, Jen stated to Kate, "I wish I had the color and length of your hair. It's so beautiful." Kate smiled.

"Thanks, Jen." Kate continued to float around the pool. She was a natural in the water.

"Is it real, or from a bottle?" Jen asked, curious. Pacey shot Jen a mean look.

"Well, that was certainly rude!" he complained. Kate laughed.

"Oh, Pacey. Women can ask each other those kinds of questions." Kate turned to Jen, answering, "Yes, Jen, my red hair is real. I'm one hundred percent Irish."

"Really, Kate? Me too!" Pacey said, latching on to any similarity.

"That's nice," Kate said, once again not really listening. She was too busy swimming and floating, enjoying the cool water. After a few minutes, she swam over to Jen and joined her by the side of the pool. She had an idea.

"Jen, I think you should use sound as your approach with Abigail and Bubbles today."

"I agree. I've already picked out my signature whistle," Jen said, proud of her research. Kate smiled, impressed.

"Great, use it all day to communicate with them. I'll bring in some calming music you can play under the water while they nap today, too."

"I have some great songs in my bag that I'd love you to try," Jen added.

"What do they sound like?" Kate asked, curious.

"Like an enchanting mermaid," Jen answered. Kate was ecstatic.

"That sounds perfect! You know, some cultures believe that mermaids are actually fallen angels. They take the shape of a dolphin or a sea lion while in the water, and switch to a human body on land. When no one is watching, they would harmonize both land and water sides together, and become a beautiful mermaid," Kate explained.

"I bet that's when the mermaid would sing her enchanting songs," Jen thought, aloud.

"The Irish call mermaids merfolk. They believe the best chance of seeing a mermaid is right before a storm. You could glimpse them sitting on a high cliff overlooking the ocean, singing to the sailors of the approaching bad weather," Kate went on to say.

"So mermaids are always good?" Jen asked.

"No, not at all," Kate answered. "Some are angry. Some intentionally use their alluring, hypnotic voices to lure sailors onto the rocks during storms, ultimately to their death."

Pacey looked over at Abigail and Bubbles. "You think one of our dolphins is a mermaid?" he asked.

Kate winked at Jen and Pacey. "Maybe. But if so, definitely a good one."

Inside the museum, Dawson and Joey found a note and a ten-dollar bill taped to Nick's office telling them to meet him down at the research vessel. Nick had taken a vehicle down to the dock an hour earlier. His only request was that Joey and

Dawson stop at Farmer Brown's Fruit Stand and grab him some breakfast.

Dawson steered as Joey rode on his bike's handlebars down the sandy road to Farmer Brown's. She kept lowering her legs, and Dawson would yell at her to lift up her feet. Joey would smile and lift them up, reminded of the scars on her knees. She had caused Dawson to tip both of them off his bike many times when they were kids. After two close calls with two large potholes and just barely missing a black snake slithering across the road, they pulled up to the fruit stand.

Farmer Brown's was a hallmark roadside fruit stand as old as Woodland Beach. It held a lot more than just fruit. There were bagels and muffins, cream cheese and lox, kiwis and papayas, tea and coffee, and much more. Farmer Brown had even caught up with the times and stocked up on protein bars and powershakes. Dawson smiled at the delicious combination of aromas pouring from its wood-slatted walls. He ordered three large coffees, three bananas, a cranberry muffin, and three toasted bagels with sweet chicken salad stuffed inside.

Joey complained that it was too much food. She was way too excited and her appetite had disappeared. But Dawson knew better and ordered the food anyway. He explained to her that they would be exerting a lot of energy during the day. Joey told Dawson to stop acting like a parent, and off they went—Joey carrying the coffees and food in her lap, trying to remember to hold up her legs, and Dawson swerving around more potholes on the road.

In less than twenty minutes, they arrived at the dock. Nick greeted Joey with a hug and went straight for the coffee and muffin.

"Thanks, you guys," he said taking a big gulp of coffee. Joey smiled. Nick seemed even cuter than before he had left for Boston. He had gotten a haircut and it looked great. Joey reached behind her back to feel her own ponytail. She was surprised how long her hair had grown over the summer. She made a mental note to ask Bessie to trim off an inch or two. Joey didn't believe in wasting hard earned money on a haircut that Bessie could easily do for free. She and Bessie had been cutting each other's hair for the last three years. Nick threw his arm around Joey, much to Dawson's not-so-hidden dismay, and directed them toward the boat.

"Ready to shove off?" Nick asked, looking at Joey. She smiled and nodded her head yes. He extended his hand and helped her aboard.

"I kind of missed you," he whispered into Joey's ear.

"I kind of missed you, too," Joey giggled back. Nick reached his hand up to Joey's ponytail and gave it a tug.

"I think you've grown since the last time I saw you," Nick teased. Joey smiled.

"A lot can happen in two days," she replied. Nick smiled at her, smitten. He wasn't lying. He had really missed this cute brunette who gave him perfect kisses. Dawson fumed. He definitely felt like a third wheel.

"I'm ready, too," said Dawson, feigning enthusiasm. "You gonna help me aboard?" Nick extended his hand a little less enthusiastically for Dawson. But Dawson didn't take it. He climbed aboard on his own. He was honestly excited for the dive but much less excited to watch Nick and Joey's constant flirtation. As Dawson stepped onto the vessel with them, Joey glanced back up the beach toward the lighthouse.

"Oh gosh, you guys . . . can you wait five more minutes?" She begged. Joey went on to explain that she had left her art supplies in the lighthouse the night before and she wanted to do some sketching while they were out on the water. None too pleased, Nick wasn't so sure. He looked at his watch, ready to say no. But then Joey looked up at him with her adorable big brown eyes, and he melted. Joey flashed a broad smile and hugged him. Then she was off in a flash, racing up the beach toward the lighthouse.

Dawson watched her go, irritated. He had just lugged Joey two miles on his handlebars, and he didn't get so much as a "Thank you!" Nick gave her one simple "Yes" and he got a smile and a hug. Life was becoming more unfair by the minute. But watching Joey run up the beach, Dawson became wistful. Joey was unusually happy today. And he liked seeing her happy. This was the summer day she had dreamed about—a day of being a part of an adventure, spending time with good friends. Dawson noticed Nick watching Joey run up the beach, too. While he was happy that Joey was happy, he wished her picture-perfect day didn't include the good-looking older guy interested in her as well. Dawson wanted to be the one to make her happy. But ever the optimist, he always held out hope that he would get his chance.

Climbing the stairs up the side of the cliff, Joey was so excited for the day ahead, she had completely forgotten about Mary. Opening the lighthouse door, she was quickly reminded. An appalling sound of crying pervaded the room. Joey cringed at the sound. She felt guilty for leaving her friend all alone.

"Mary, don't cry," Joey pleaded, looking around for a sign of her. But the crying continued. Mary was angry at Joey for planning to leave her alone all day. Joey explained that she'd be back to play tomorrow. She even promised to draw a beautiful picture while out on the water, and hang it up in the lighthouse. Mary didn't care. Her crying continued as Joey packed up her art supplies. Joey wished Mary would grow up and understand that she had a life beyond the lighthouse and Woodland Beach. "I'll be back," she assured the child ghost. As Joey locked the door to leave, a breeze rolled into the room and the crying died away.

"Oh," Joey gasped. Down the cliff, Joey saw what

appeared to be roses. Someone had actually picked the blooms and placed them like markers on the cliff, across the dunes, across the beach, and out into the ocean. Joey followed the flowers in wonder, breathing in their scent. Joey hoped it was a sign from Mary, giving Joey her blessing to venture out into the sea. "A-choo!" Joey sneezed, then laughed. "They're beautiful," she called out. A warm breeze seemed to wrap itself around her.

Back at the dock, Joey climbed onto the research vessel and slipped her life vest over her head. Maneuvering over the rolling waves, Nick motored out to sea. Anxious to catch up with Joey, he struggled to remain focused on his map coordinates and the ocean. Dawson, full of energy and caffeine, began separating their scuba equipment. Tired from her quick sprint up and down the cliff, Joey sat down on the hull to eat her chicken salad sandwich.

"Hey, Nick," she asked. "How long until we get there?"

Nick looked at his watch. "About thirty minutes, give or take a little," he answered. Since it would be a good half-hour before they were at their designated diving spot, Joey pulled out her art supplies. She glanced back at the shore as she enjoyed the rest of her sandwich and the sound of the ocean. Maybe she would sketch the lighthouse for Mary. Joey opened up the case that contained her pastels and noticed that one was missing. She looked around on the floor of the vessel to see if it had slipped out of the case. It wasn't there. Joey sighed. Her chalks were expensive and she hated to lose one.

As Joey opened her drawing pad to sketch, a familiar aroma swept up from between the crisp, white pages. It was the sweet perfume of a full flowering rose. Joey smiled, remembering the path of blooms Mary had laid out for her, then sneezed two times in a row. She borrowed Dawson's binoculars, wanting one last view of the beautiful floral path she had just traipsed down. Peering through the lenses, Joey's smile quickly faded. She watched in horror as the roses withered away to brown crisps on the sand—and then, into nothingness. It was a definite warning from Mary for Joey not to go. Joey turned her head away from shore, angry at her little ghost friend. She refused to be bullied. There was something deep inside of her that told her she had to do this dive. No matter what the cost.

Almost to their destination, Dawson took over maneuvering the boat, while Nick and Joey put on their wet suits and scuba tanks. Joey and Nick laughed as they got ready. Dawson couldn't help but notice the romantic sparks between them. Nick was driven by his love for the sea, just as Dawson was driven by his love for film. But Dawson was driven by something else as well—his love for Joey. He hoped that it wouldn't be something he and Nick had in common. But that internal drive, whether for the sea or film, appealed to someone like Joey, who just hadn't quite found her own passion yet. And then there was the fact that Nick possessed a few minor things Dawson didn't—a college diploma, a smile straight out of a Colgate ad, and a passport with stamps from more than ten countries.

Joey called to Dawson. "Dawson, I think we're here." Nick nodded in agreement.

"This is it," he said. "This should be the spot." Dawson stopped the boat and dropped the anchor overboard. He had decided it would be better if one person stayed on the vessel. Also, he could videotape the event. And if all went well, Kate had guaranteed Dawson use of the museum's underwater camera to come back and film the ship before it was raised. But actually, Dawson was mostly in the mood to sulk. Watching Joey and Nick flirt had bothered him, and he didn't want to go down into the water for another hour and a half to watch it some more.

Nick thought it might have been helpful to have an extra diver, but he also knew he and Joey would be enthusiastic enough for all three of them. With time of the essence, he chose not to argue about whether Dawson joined them or stayed on the vessel. The main thing was to get going! Nick instructed Dawson about the boat and then lowered himself into the water. Joey was right behind him. Dawson began filming as soon as they hit the water.

Through his camera's lens, Dawson watched Joey and Nick prepare for their dive. Nick helped Joey with her tank, making the appropriate final adjustments. Dawson wished he was the one helping her. But, lucky pennies and wishes weren't getting him very far. So, instead of wasting time wishing, he adjusted his lens, and focused on the task at hand. Dawson was going to spend his next hour and a half coming up with a new strategy.

Finished, Nick looked at Joey and smiled. "Ready to find the ship?" he asked. Dog-paddling, Joey gave him her divers "thumbs up!"

"Definitely." She smiled. Joey imagined sitting at Bessie's computer later, doctoring her résumé. Forget yearbook, student government, and the honor society. Under "additional information" she could put "recovering historic ship wreckage" — that would certainly make her résumé memorable. College admissions offices everywhere would perk up and take notice. It wouldn't be every day a "Jackie" Cousteau résumé landed on their desks.

Joey and Nick waved to the camera, pulled down their masks and together, ducked under the water. Less than a minute later, they were completely out of sight.

Under the water, Joey hurried to keep up with Nick, who immediately began searching the ocean floor for a sign of the wreckage. Often he would point in one direction and they would separate briefly, each swimming in a different part of the water. But Nick was sure to keep an eye on Joey and Joey on Nick.

Nick was diving about thirty feet lower than Joey

and the ocean floor was about thirty feet below that. He had more diving experience and decided it would be better for Joey if she went no more than twenty-five feet down. Sometimes the pressure could make a person light-headed, and make a diver lose all sense of direction. Also, if Joey had any problems underwater, Nick wanted her to be relatively close to the surface. Coming up too fast from so far below could be dangerous, and he didn't want to put Joey in a situation she couldn't handle. So she swam above him as he scanned the ocean floor, desperately hoping to find the ship.

At first, Joey was having trouble focusing on looking for the ship's remains. The bottom of the ocean was cloudy, and the water was busy with activity. Schools of fish were constantly swimming by her, changing direction as if on a whim. Joey watched, intrigued, as a large silver fish swam out of some seaweed and swallowed a little rainbow fish whole. And three fat gold fish even had the nerve to bubble by her and poke at her mask. She wanted to laugh but her mask wouldn't allow for much facial movement.

Joey was fully enjoying her dive as the ocean continued to impress her. Even amidst all the activity, it was so beautifully peaceful and serene. Sucking oxygen in and out of her tube, the air sounded cold and hollow. Joey wished she had an underwater video camera because she would never be able to describe this world to her family or friends. She remembered her mother saying she had been snorkeling once, before she was diagnosed with breast cancer. She always had told Joey that someday they would explore the ocean underwater together. It was just one more dream that had not been fulfilled.

Nick seemed to be getting more frantic as the dive wore on. He was desperate to find the Breckinridge wreckage. He had been sure this was the spot, but nothing indicated the presence of an old ship. Nick gestured that they should separate one more time before heading back up. But something was unsettling to Joey. She just didn't feel as if they were in the right spot. She didn't know what or where the right spot was, she just knew that this didn't feel like this was it.

Joey checked her watch. It was almost time for them to leave. Another gold-colored fish swam by her. Joey hung motionless as the underwater waves rocked her body back and forth. Joey's mind drifted from her mother, to the sea, to Mary. She wondered if there would be sunken treasure in the broken ship—with gold coins, rich jewels, and silver trinkets. Maybe they would find pieces of furniture, clothes, or sadly, toys. Would there be skeletons still on board? Joey's mind shuddered at the thought.

Joey must have passed directly under the boat, because suddenly there were shadows all around her in the water. One of them was Nick's image. It was time for them to go. Even underwater, Joey could see the disappointment in Nick's eyes. He gestured Joey to head up. They had not found the ship or any hint of the wreckage.

Dawson filmed Joey and Nick slowly swimming up to the surface. Halfway up, Joey's leg began to cramp. Dawson, anxiously capturing the moment, was thankful he had made her eat a banana, in addition to her chicken salad, before the dive. Without the added potassium in her body, the leg cramp could have been much worse.

Nick quickly swam over to help Joey. She pointed to her leg and Nick rubbed the muscle until it stopped violently contracting. She nodded that it felt better. She pointed "up" and they began swimming toward the surface.

Dawson continued to film Joey and Nick as they swam up to the top, hand in hand. A familiar jealousy rose up inside him. He wanted to be the romantic hero in the water rubbing Joey's leg and holding her hand. Not the friend up in the boat who fed her the banana before she went down. Dawson stopped filming, allowing himself to be swept up in one big massive swirl of anger.

Joey and Nick were holding hands when they broke through the surface of the water. Joey could see Dawson in the boat. She tried waving to him with her free hand, but he didn't respond. She wondered why he wasn't filming them. Instead, he was staring at them like his mind was a million miles away. Suddenly, a brilliant light surrounded Dawson's image.

Joey watched as Dawson's face distorted into Mary's. But it wasn't the angelic face of the sweet English girl that she'd played with up at the lighthouse. This Mary's face was filled with jealousy and hate. Joey watched Mary's image turn even more hideous, yet she couldn't pull her eyes away. This was an angry Mary Breckinridge.

Joey jerked back from the boat. She didn't want to face this ghost's jealousies, anger, and hate. Joey's mask came loose over her nose and eyes and a wave sloshed over her face, water entering her mask. Joey choked and gagged, panicky. A hand reached behind her and pulled her back to reality.

When Nick reached the boat with Joey in his arms, Dawson was relieved. "Hey!" Dawson exclaimed. "What just happened? I was starting to wonder if you guys were ever coming back."

Joey shook her head, coughing, the air coming back into her lungs. With Nick's help, she climbed up the ladder and onto the side of the vessel. "Me, too," she said quietly. Nick had swum after her and forced her up into the boat. Joey blamed her odd behavior on her leg cramp.

"How long were we down for?" Joey asked as Dawson helped her up into the boat.

Dawson looked at his watch, but Nick already knew the correct answer. "About an hour and a half," he said disappointed, throwing his gear over into the boat.

"It felt like five hours," Dawson commented. He looked at Joey, his jealousy subsiding, and his worry setting in. "Look at your hands," he said to Joey as he reached out and pulled them into his. Joey looked down. Her fingers were all pruned up, like raisins. She shuddered at them, reminded of Mary's awful face. Dawson could sense something had happened in the water.

"Are you okay, Joe?" Dawson asked her, concerned.

"Sure, I'm fine, I just had a little cramp. I'll be fine." Joey didn't want to talk about Mary. She was still in shock. Dawson led Joey over to the side of the boat. They sat down.

"So," Dawson asked, hopeful, changing the subject, "Any luck?" Dawson's questions only worsened the depressing mood on the boat.

Nick walked over and handed Joey her bag of clothes. He shook his head. "No. Afraid not."

Nick and Joey peeled off their wet suits and changed clothes, while Dawson continued to capture some remaining footage of their location. Joey quickly slipped on jeans and a sweatshirt as Nick finished changing. He stared down into the ocean, speechless with disappointment. Finally, he looked up at Joey. He had tears in his eyes and she got equally choked up. He reached out and hugged her. She felt light-headed, like she might pass out again. Together, they hugged each other for comfort.

Dawson put the camera down, and looked the other way. He had learned his lesson about trying to dictate Joey's actions—he wasn't about to stop her, but that didn't mean he had to watch. He was shaken by the intense feelings of anger and jealousy watching Joey and Nick together. It felt like it wasn't him, like someone had taken over his mind—into a dark place that he never wanted to go back to again. It was not the Dawson Wade Leery that he wanted to be.

Finally, they were ready to head in for the day. Back at the helm, Nick maneuvered the boat toward shore. Sensing Nick needed some time alone, Joey walked to the back of the boat and sat down beside Dawson. He was watching the footage he'd just filmed.

Joey laughed at the funny home movie. Starting out on the trip, she had been camera shy for about two seconds until she realized there was no chance Dawson wasn't going to film the entire expedition. Whether she liked it or not, Dawson had cast her as the female lead.

Joey and Dawson watched the video together. She was sketching for a while and Dawson zoomed in on the image. After that, he had captured Joey listening intently as Nick spoke of his love for the sea. She looked at him as if he possessed the answer to the meaning of life.

Joey was embarrassed by the film. "Okay, fast forward over the sickening summer crush scene," she urged. Dawson fast-forwarded the footage, appreciating not having to watch it for the second time today. It had been painful enough to watch Joey's fascination with Nick the first time. But he couldn't help but smile, at Joey's calling Nick her "summer crush." Maybe Jen had been right in suggesting that's all Joey and Nick's romance was.

Next, Joey and Dawson watched the footage of Joey and Nick diving underwater. Dawson's voice could be heard in the background giving a running commentary on their surroundings. Dawson had zoomed his camera in on Manor Light in the distance, retelling the legend for posterity. The image pulled out from the jetty and over to the dock, from which they had set sail. It zoomed in on the dock and—

"Wait a minute," Joey interrupted the viewing. "What's that?" Dawson looked at the image.

"The dock," he answered. Joey shook her head.

"No, no," she said. "Beyond the dock, by the tree." Dawson looked more closely. Next to the tree, there was clearly a little girl.

Dawson shook his head. "There's no way . . . There was no one there when I filmed this. I swear," he insisted. Joey's eyes widened, taking in the image.

"Dawson, that's her," she exclaimed, adamant. "That's Mary Breckinridge—the girl who I've been seeing."

Usually, Dawson would have been skeptical. Usually he would have launched into an explanation, saying Joey was letting her imagination run wild. But he knew no one had been around that tree while he was taping. He knew, because he had taped it. On the video, he talked about the tree and Joey's fears. He even zoomed in to see if he could find the "X" carved into the tree. There had been no little girl standing there. But now, looking at the footage, there was no doubt—she was there.

When the research vessel docked, Dawson hopped off quickly. Joey said a quick "thank you" to Nick and the two took off running toward the lighthouse. Joey wasn't sure why she didn't tell Nick about their suspicion. Maybe it was his sadness, and her not wanting to bother him. Or maybe she just enjoyed the comfort of having Dawson finally believe her.

Joey ran fast, with Dawson right on her heels. She had to go to the lighthouse. Something was drawing her there. When they got up the hill, they burst in the door. Joey looked up and screamed. On the far wall, the angry words "PLAY WITH ME" were scrawled in a child's bad penmanship. At first glance Joey thought it was written in blood, but when she got closer she realized it had been written with one of her red oil chalks from her art case. Joey hadn't misplaced the missing pastel; Mary had stolen it.

Joey slowly walked toward the wall, entranced. Something was resting at its base. She leaned down and picked up a ragged doll. Its hair was fringed from fire. Its dress tattered and torn. Joey looked at it, flipping the doll over as if inspecting it for clues. Then something caught her eye. On the bottom of a foot was sewn "Mary B."

"Dawson, look." Joey handed him the doll. Dawson inspected it slowly.

"Is this . . . ?" He was almost afraid to ask.

"Mary Breckinridge?" Joey answered his question before he asked it. "It's really her, Dawson. She's here."

Dawson couldn't believe it. He had a hard enough time believing that there was actually a sunken ship for them to find. Now he was supposed to believe that this little girl was . . . here. Haunting them. He tried to think logically but . . . Subterranean caves don't cause a little doll to suddenly appear in a lighthouse. Something was definitely going on.

"Okay, let's think about what you claim has happened." he said.

"Not what I claim has happened. What *has* happened." Joey interrupted. Maybe she should have asked Nick to come up to the lighthouse with them. But then again, she had run back to get her chalks before they had pushed off to sail. Maybe she had written the words on the wall and put the doll in the lighthouse herself. Maybe she was losing her mind.

Joey walked over to the wall and began erasing the words with her shirt sleeve. But it wasn't rubbing off. Joey was desperate to have this all go away. She twirled around the room screaming up into the light tower. "Do you hear me, Mary? I don't want to play with you anymore. I won't play with you anymore! I don't know how to help you!"

Dawson watched her, worried. He saw how Joey had run toward the lighthouse, seemingly against her will. The experience had left him shaken. Something was happening to her, and it wasn't in her mind. He walked over to Joey and put his arms around her. He was going to help her. Joey looked into Dawson's confident eyes.

"What do I do, Dawson? Tell, me. What do I do?" Dawson answered Joey simply. "We see if Mary takes no for an answer." A small smile emerged on Joey's face. No matter how much black-and-white he saw, she could always count on Dawson to reject reality with her, even just for an afternoon.

As they walked down to the beach, Joey took comfort in Dawson's energy. He was busy putting the pieces together, forming his plan on how to get rid of Mary. Dawson continued to ask Joey questions.

"You say there was the compass—"

"—mysteriously pointing southeast," Joey finished.

"What else?" Dawson tried to remember.

"The 'X' on the tree," Joey reminded him. "Which Mary kept pointing to—"

"Now the doll and the name sewn on," Dawson said thoughtfully. Joey sighed. Dawson was trying to find the logic in the situation, but there was no logic.

"Dawson, forget what's real and what makes

sense. I mean, sometimes things happen that we can't understand—like my mom dying and my dad going to prison." She tried to appeal to his sense of confusion about his own life. "Like your parents' divorce. Like us."

"Joey, you can't compare the two." Dawson reasoned. He was surprised that Joey would bring up their relationship but didn't think that this was the time to pursue it.

"Why not?" Joey continued. "My gut is asking me to figure out what is the one thing Mary Breckinridge would want."

Dawson looked at Joey, stone faced. "I think that's pretty obvious." Joey frowned, discouraged. They had come full circle to the one thing Joey was sick of hearing.

"I don't want to play with Mary Breckinridge anymore. I'm tired and it's no longer fun."

"Then if she doesn't take no for an answer, we'll make her stop!" Dawson said, adamantly.

8

The Lighthouse Legend

"Absolutely, positively, indubitably NOT! Nope, not gonna happen!" Pacey firmly planted his foot into the wet sand, leaving a footprint. The afternoon had turned windy and cold despite the sun shining down on the water. Having walked out of the lighthouse with a solid plan, Joey and Dawson were standing on the beach trying to talk Pacey into something that he did not want any part of.

"Come on, Pacey. We need your help," Dawson urged. "Joey needs your help." Joey looked up at Pacey with her big brown eyes. Pacey was a sucker for those pleading puppy eyes. But not this time. Those brown eyes could only get her so far. This was where he drew the line.

Pacey flipped his black Oakleys over his eyes and answered, "NOT!" He turned toward the water. Board in hand, he had been hoping to do a little surfing. Jen had found the old surfboard while hiding in the shed with Dawson playing flashlight tag. Together he, Kate, and Jen had sanded it down, and fixed it up. Although he hadn't scored with Kate, the natural beauty thought highly of him. And who knew, ten years from now, it could be a whole new ball game. . . .

Pacey stared out at the waves. They were breaking nicely. It was a perfect afternoon for a good ride. Not that he knew how to have a good ride. But he figured it couldn't be all that difficult. He saw people on the beach all the time, boards gliding over the water effortlessly. How hard could it be? Put the leash on the wrist, jump on the board, hop up on it, and ride it in. Joey laughed, amused at something.

"What?" Pacey questioned. "Something funny, Potter?" Joey undid the leash from Pacey's wrist.

"It's supposed to strap to your ankle, Pacey," she said. Pacey shrugged, embarrassed.

"I knew that," he lied. Pacey reached down and strapped the leash to his ankle. Dawson laughed.

"Since you're right-handed, I'm guessing you should probably be putting it on your other ankle," he advised. Pacey ripped the leash off his ankle. He was getting sick of their critique. "Everyone's an expert, huh?" Pacey shook his head. Desperately needing some time to chill, he stared out at the ocean, wanting to jump in and let off some steam.

Joey and Dawson stood there, giving him his space. They knew Pacey would eventually come around. It might not be until he was starving or needed to be let out, but he would come around. In the last few days, Pacey had worked harder than he had in his whole life. Even harder than when he helped the Potters get the B&B up and running. Four lighthouse tours and added aquarium duties due to Bubbles's birth—Pacey was physically tired and emotionally spent. Pacey dropped his board and waded out into the water to do a little body surfing. If he couldn't stand up on the board, he could at least catch some waves on his belly and tan his back in the process.

Dawson and Joey waited for an answer. Pacey didn't want to give into them but he was a little curious. "What time would it take place? And exactly what would it entail?" Pacey asked. Dawson and Joey smiled. They were wearing him down.

"Oh, you'd have plenty of time to catch a few waves," Joey tempted.

"Sure," Dawson agreed.

"And . . . ?" Pacey probed. He wanted all the specifics. What exactly did the two of them have in mind? Dawson walked down to the oceanfront to give Pacey a long, complicated lecture on their plan to get rid of Mary. "First, we go get Jen to agree. Then we're going to the museum, to jump online and look for the right—"

"Séance mumbo jumbo . . . No biggie though,"

Joey spit out, quickly, as she dragged Dawson down the beach toward the aquarium. Pacey had just agreed, and she didn't want Dawson messing it up with further details. Dawson, quickly picking up his pace, ran beside Joey. He liked her strategy.

"See you at sundown," Dawson yelled to Pacey. Wading in the water, Pacey watched them run off down the beach.

"Order a pizza—from Peppinos," he called after them. Pacey was going to milk this Scooby-Do adventure for all it was worth. "And make it a pepperoni with lots of extra cheese." He would need some "Scooby snacks" to make it through the séance. His stomach growl was known to wake the dead.

In the distance, Joey grabbed Dawson's hand and the two of them ran through the waves, toward the aquarium, enjoying the surf.

"Thanks, Dawson," Joey said. Dawson squeezed Joey's hand tightly. It felt good helping her.

Jen was standing in the pool feeding Bubbles from a bottle under Kate's watchful eye. Abigail's weakened immune system had made her unable to nurse. And Abigail hated it. Initially, she had swam circles around Bubbles while Jen would feed her. But unable to control her disappointment, she sulked off to the side of the pool. Jen hated that Abigail was distancing herself.

As Jen was trying to think of a way to reconnect Abigail with her baby, Joey and Dawson burst into the room, on a mission. Abigail began lapping the pool, disturbed at the sight of Joey. Abigail's movement was making Bubbles uneasy. Kate marched right over to Abigail, and in a very firm voice told her, "Settle down!" Abigail quieted, but kept her distance at the other end of the pool as Kate walked around to check out the agitated mother. Kate, who was feeling a little agitated herself, sat down on the side of the pool. She put her hand to her forehead, feeling feverish and flushed. At the other end of the pool, Jen climbed out, surprised to see the two of them.

"What's up?" she questioned.

"A séance," Dawson answered. Jen laughed.

"Yeah, right. Tell me another one." But Dawson and Joey weren't laughing. They were standing in front of her, arms crossed and dead serious. Jen picked up a towel and began drying off.

"And a dose of reality hasn't kicked in yet, because . . . ?" Jen was still convinced Joey's voice and vision of Mary Breckinridge was all in her head. If anyone deserved to have an imaginary friend help her through some hard issues, it was Joey. But this was crazy. A séance was going one step too far.

"Joey," Jen asked cautiously, "have you ever thought of seeing someone?"

"Seeing someone?" Joey didn't get where Jen was going with this.

"My Grams . . ." Jen continued, "she knows a lot of people . . . professionals . . . well trained professionals. . . ." Jen wasn't sure if Joey was catching her drift.

Suddenly, Joey's confusion turned to anger. "Are you suggesting I see a shrink?"

"I'll drive you," Jen offered.

Joey took a deep breath and counted to ten. "Look," she said, "with what I've been through in the past seventeen years, I'm sure professional help could be a useful tool. But this has nothing to do with my mental state. There are facts that point to that lighthouse being haunted, and since I'm the one that spends the majority of my day in there, I don't care what you think. So back off with the psychoanalysis and make yourself useful!" Joey stormed off, irate.

Shocked at Joey's passionate words, Jen appealed to Dawson. "Joey needs therapy, not a séance," Jen said, matter-of-factly.

"Joey, wait!" Dawson called out. Joey turned around.

"Jen, look." Dawson had a way to convince the unconvincable. He pulled his video camera out of his bag to show her the video of the mysterious little girl standing by the tree.

"So what? A girl by a tree?" Jen wasn't sold. "You've been known to have quite an imaginative mind, too, Dawson," she reasoned. Joey walked back over to them. In the meantime, Kate had removed her socks and shoes and was dangling her feet into the water. She listened as the three kids argued.

"I'm telling you, Jen, that little girl wasn't standing by that tree when I filmed this footage," Dawson insisted. Dawson pushed a button on the recorder to rewind. He wanted Jen to look at the little girl again. But Dawson hit forward instead. The tape ended up circling back to the very first footage he had taken at Woodland Beach. It was the afternoon that Jen had pushed Pacey into the pool. Quietly, while the others were engrossed with the video, Kate gathered up her socks and shoes and slipped out the back door.

"Hey, wait a minute!" Joey said, as the tape automatically started playing.

"Oh, my God!" Dawson said, watching the image appear on the tape.

Jen glanced at the screen on the camera. It was the image Dawson had unknowingly captured that first day in the aquarium. It was the image of little Mary Breckinridge. Not the beautiful, shimmering soul Joey had been playing with on the beach. This was Mary as she really was. A little English girl— her gray face bloated, long blond hair matted with seaweed, and her white dress tattered with blood and gravel. Dawson zoomed the camera in for a closer look. All were horrified to see Mary's cold, terrifying eyes staring intently at Joey. Speechless, Jen looked at Dawson. "If this is some sort of joke, Dawson . . ." Jen's voice trailed off. Dawson shook his head.

With the video as proof, Jen cut Pacey's surfing break short. He was needed by Joey . . . and as the three went off to prepare for the long night ahead, once again, Pacey was designated as chore boy. At the moment, he was cleaning out the largest pool in the aquarium, Abigail's pool. Usually friendly, she was still depressed and distancing herself from Bubbles. Pacey looked at the temperamental dolphin.

"Yeah, I know exactly how you feel." Pacey frowned, scooping an uneaten herring out of the pool.

"And how is that?" Kate asked, curiously. She had walked into the aquarium to check on things, before calling it a day. She still wasn't feeling quite herself.

"Tired and lousy," Pacey said, depressed. Kate smiled, excited.

"Perfect, Pacey. That's perfect!" Kate screamed in joy. Pacey was confused.

"Did you hear me correctly?" Pacey asked. "I said that I feel tired and lousy," he said, his voice a little louder.

"Yes, I heard you," Kate said, rushing over to the divers' pool. She grabbed a scuba tank and dragged it over to the pool. Pacey walked over to help her.

"And that's a good thing . . . because?" Pacey asked.

"Oh, well, I guess the lousy part isn't very good," Kate said, distracted. She rushed over to other side of the pool and pulled down a few large rafts from the top of a shelf. Pacey followed behind her to help.

"But the tired part is okay? Why?" Pacey was still in the dark.

"When you said you were tired, that gave me an idea," Kate continued. She was dragging the rafts over to the side of the pool. She hooked up the scuba's oxygen tank to one and began filling it with air. Pacey watched the large raft fill up, and smiled. He knew what was going on. He had won his siren over. His face was filled with bravado.

"Oh, I get it. You've been looking for a reason to sleep with me. Well, sure, Kate, we can take a little nappy-nap together." Pacey reached over and grabbed a raft and started blowing it up with all his might. Kate doubled over in laughter.

"Not exactly, Pacey. You see, I want you to take a nap with Abigail." Pacey stopped blowing up his raft. Okay, even a Witter had limits. Kate shook her head at Pacey's perplexed look.

"A real nap, Pacey. No nappy-nap. A real nap!"

"Oh," Pacey said relieved, continuing to blow up the raft. The request sinking in, he stopped. "Why?"

"Because I think Abigail's worked herself into such a state of depression, she's not sleeping," Kate advised. She threw a few rafts into the water. "Grab one of Abigail's Hula-Hoops from her toy chest and some long rope from the nets." Pacey did as he was instructed. He helped Kate tie six long strings to the Hula-Hoop. Afterward, he connected the opposite ends of five of the strings to five individual rafts. When Pacey had finished, Kate threw the huge community floating device into the water. Suddenly, Kate turned white as a ghost, all the color draining out of her face.

"Kate?" Pacey asked, concerned. "You all right?" Kate suddenly seemed distracted and uncomfortable. Her hands were trembling. Shaking, she stripped down to her bathing suit and cautiously climbed into the water. As soon as she entered the pool, her face regained its normal color, her cheeks becoming rosy again, and the trembling stopped.

"Wow," Pacey said. "Water has quite an effect on you."

"Come on in. Hop on a raft, and lets nap," Kate encouraged. Pacey had been watching Kate walk around in her bathing suit. He wasn't quite up for a nap any longer. No, Pacey was wide awake.

"I'd rather have a cold shower," he said, under his breath. Pacey climbed into the pool and onto a raft.

A few minutes later, Jen, Joey, and Dawson returned to the aquarium, having completed their séance preparations. One of Jen's tranquil songs was playing in the room. The jets in the water were turning the community floating device in a circling motion, and Kate and Pacey were both sound asleep. The three laughed at Pacey and Kate's "nap-on-your-raft-around-the-merry-Hula-Hoop." Pacey stirred at the sound.

"C'mon in guys, and join us for a nap. We're trying to make Abigail undepressed. It hasn't worked for her, but it's doing wonders for me. Oh, and be quiet, Kate's asleep," Pacey said, with a yawn.

Jen looked at her watch; it was still two hours before sundown. They had time. At her nod of approval, Joey and Dawson undressed to their swimsuits and they all climbed into the pool. Each of them grabbing their own raft, they eagerly joined the aquatic merry-go-round.

"I don't get it," Dawson said.

"Yeah, how is this going to get Abigail to be undepressed?" Joey questioned.

"Beats me," answered Pacey. "I'm just following orders."

An hour later, after everyone had drifted off to sleep, the one watching pair of eyes in the room looked on in delight, as Abigail swam over and hooked her mouth to the only rope hanging empty from the Hula-Hoop. Abigail had connected herself to their herd. And in doing so, she would begin to accept their help with Bubbles. But their five-person raft and one dolphin merry-go-round was not quite complete. Jen smiled when little Bubbles swam over to Abigail to join her. Abigail held her little baby's fin with hers and finally began to feel like Mom.

At sundown, Joey, Dawson, Jen, and Pacey walked up the beach. Stopping at the cliff, Pacey looked up at the lighthouse. Its lone window was dark and gray. The bird's nest on its ledge sat empty. A lone crow silently circled the top of the watchtower, warning them not to come closer. The ocean rolled with a wild intensity. And the dark clouds above were hanging low, trying to smother the beach.

"Manor Light doesn't look very inviting!" Pacey gulped.

"Well, someone knows we're coming," Joey said, noticing a trail of wilted roses leading up to the lighthouse. Jen picked up a wilted bloom and tossed it into a big braided bag she was carrying.

"This should help," Jen said. Dawson walked over and pointed out the oak tree.

"Here's the 'X,'" he said to Jen. Jen walked over and carved some wood off the tree, and dropped it into her bag.

"This should work, too," Jen exclaimed. Joey quickly ran down to the ocean and filled a small glass jar with seawater. Closing the lid tightly, she walked back up to the gang.

"Is that everything?" Joey asked. Jen pulled a list from out of her bag and checked it.

"Everything from out here," Jen said.

Gathering their courage, Dawson, Joey and Jen headed up to the lighthouse. Still at the bottom, Pacey stared at the tall monument, worried. "I'm telling you guys, this place doesn't look very inviting!" he complained. "Why don't we just sit right here, do a quick round of 'light-as-a-feather-stiff-as-a-board' and call it a day?" Dawson walked back down, and gently prodded Pacey up the hill. Pacey complained all the way. "Fine. Fine. But if movie horror history is correct, you do realize that Jen and myself will be the first to go!" Dawson looked at Pacey confused.

"And why is that, Pace?" he questioned.

"Didn't you see *Scream*? The creepy antagonist always kills off the sexually promiscuous first," Pacey explained.

"While they're in bed, having sex! And that won't be happening, Pacey," Jen rebuked. "Anyway, they do that to show breast cleavage, not for plot points." Joey looked down at the wilted flowers leading the way to Manor Light. She sighed, worried.

"I guess that makes me the virginal offering," Joey frowned. Jen put her arm around Joey, comfortingly.

"No, it makes you smart," Jen said. "Besides, you'll have to compete with Dawson for virginal status."

Joey gave Dawson a quick kiss on the cheek as she joined him on the cliff, "If it looks like we won't make it out of here alive, we'll have a quickie." Dawson smiled. Thoughts of a quickie with Joey could definitely get him through this séance.

The sun dipped down over the horizon, there was no moon in the sky, and it was officially night. Dawson and Joey led the way into the lighthouse, with Jen and Pacey following behind. All began working diligently to prepare for their séance.

Dawson lit the lanterns, passed out flashlights and pepper spray. Pacey opened up his pizza box and starting eating.

"Pepper spray?" Pacey laughed. "What are you planning to do to Mary? Give her an allergy attack?" Pacey, gulping a slice of pizza, rolled out a loud burp.

"Some of us aren't so fortunate as to be equipped with such deadly gases," Dawson commented, hooking his pepper spray to his pants pocket.

Meanwhile, Jen and Joey were busy arranging for the séance. Jen laid out a large handkerchief, and placed all of Mary's earthly materials in it. "This should help us to call up her spirit," Jen advised. Joey looked at all the items: the rag doll, a piece of bark from the "X" on the tree, Joey's artwork which Mary had colored in, the wilted rose, and—

"We're missing the compass," Joey said. Dawson unhooked it from the wall and brought it over and laid it in the middle of the objects. Jen placed two cards on each end. YES on the south corner. NO on the north corner.

"Okay, let's begin," Jen said, sitting down. The group formed a circle around the compass. A storm began outside, as Jen began the séance. Following an old book of spells, she read a century-old nursery rhyme and sprinkled the ocean water over all of the items.

"I bet you were a riot at slumber parties," Pacey laughed. He continued to make witty small talk from nerves, until Dawson unhooked his pepper spray and threatened to use it. Jen continued, as Joey stared intently at the compass.

"Is there anyone in this room other than the four of us?" Jen asked.

The compass swung to YES!

Everyone was spooked. Pacey would have leaped out the door if it wasn't for Jen's tight grip on his thigh. "Is your name Mary Breckinridge?" Jen continued.

Again, the compass swung to YES!

Everyone took a deep breath, for they knew what Jen's next question would be.

"Will you please leave our friend, Joey, alone?" she asked.

The compass swung to NO!

Joey looked over at the wall. Mary's red writing, PLAY WITH ME was still ingrained there. Joey spoke up, determined to have all this end. "I don't want to play with you anymore, Mary. You have to accept that."

The compass swung wildly around and landed back on NO!

Over and over and over again . . . it kept pointing to NO! Mary wanted Joey to play with her and she wouldn't accept "no" for an answer. Joey tried to talk to Mary like she had on the beach.

"Mary, why don't you go find your mom on the beach and play with her?" Joey asked. "If I could, I would play with my mom."

The compass flickered, unable to answer. Jen thought of Abigail being lost from her herd. "Do you know where your parents are, Mary?" Jen asked.

The compass spun wildly around. The spinning was so fast and intense, it seemed as if the needle might separate from the rest of the apparatus.

Joey understood where Jen was going with her line of questioning. Jen continued. "Do you know what happened to your parents, Mary? Do you know what happened to you?" she asked.

The compass spun wildly for another moment and then began to go slower and slower until finally, it settled on NO.

Jen continued to ask questions and soon they were able to piece Mary's answers into a story that made sense. The truth was, Mary was a true lost soul. Washed away from her parents' bodies, she had been wandering around restless, not able to find her home. And as time wore on, she became angry at her parents for leaving her all alone, for abandoning her. For letting her slide off their boat and into the dark water alone.

Joey said softly to Mary, "I know you don't understand all that's happened to you. But you have to know your parents would never have chosen to let you go."

The compass started to tremble. Joey continued. "In fact, they could be looking for you now, just like you're looking for them."

"What does she want?" Pacey asked, frustrated. "Us to find her parents for her?"

The compass moved to YES.

Joey spoke softly, "Mary, we don't know how to help you." As Joey spoke, a quiet weeping filled the lighthouse. They were all helpless, trying to fit pieces of a puzzle together, but so far nothing was matching up. Finally, a lonely gust of wind swept into the room and the sad weeping sailed away. Everyone stood in silence, in disbelief, in relief, and in some way saddened. It seemed that the séance was over and Mary Breckinridge was gone.

As they gathered their things to leave, the door to the lighthouse slammed shut, locking them in. The compass needle began circling wildly. Everyone came back and stared at the compass. That feeling of dread that Joey knew only to well, swept up around her. The needle kept circling angrily. The lighthouse stones began to crack. And the weather outside began to rage. Once again, Jen, remaining calm amidst the storm, was reminded of Abigail and Bubbles. Like Bubbles, maybe Mary was scared to venture out into the scary sea alone. Maybe she needed mothering.

"Do you want us to take you to your parents?" Jen asked.

The compass slowed, and swiveled to YES.

Joey frowned. "But we don't know where that is, Mary. We've been looking, but we can't find it."

The compass swiveled to SOUTHEAST.

The glass face of the compass shattered, as Dawson looked down at the signaled direction and had an idea. "Maybe that's it," Dawson said jumping up excited. "Maybe we need to sail southeast."

"You need more than a direction," Pacey said, knowingly. "You need coordinates."

"Wait a minute," Joey said, remembering the numbers hidden in the wallpaper. "Could those numbers be coordinates? Maybe that's where the ship went down."

"How would Mary know the coordinates?" Dawson asked.

"How would Mary be communicating with us?" Pacey fired back.

"Logic went out the window a long time ago." Joey agreed.

"Maybe it's someone else besides Mary," Dawson reasoned.

"Like who?" Jen asked.

Joey thought for a moment. The answer was suddenly obvious. "Her parents," Joey said.

Mary's joyous laughter could be heard throughout the room. "Will you take me to my parents, Josephine?" Everyone looked on, stunned. Jen was right, this was what Mary wanted.

Joey answered, softly, smiling, "Yes, Mary, I'll take you." The lighthouse door creaked open.

While the foursome was up in the lighthouse figuring out how to help Mary, Nick paced the beach below. He stared at the research vessel intently, as he was running numbers in his head, going over his research again and again. Nick glanced up at the lighthouse. He had spied Joey and her gang going up there an hour earlier. But it had only been a momentary distraction. Nothing they were doing could be more important than what he cared about most—finding the sunken wreckage. He had gone over the same map twenty times in the last few hours. Nick sighed. He was running out of time.

Meanwhile, Pacey and Jen cleaned up the light-house, as Dawson and Joey were in the watchtower mapping a nautical chart. Using tools from the museum, Dawson's research and Joey's colored chalks, they plotted out distance points, ocean depths, riptides, and the rocky coastline. Joey's Lighthouse Legend seemingly solved, they were ready to make another dive.

"What's that? Joey asked, looking out the window to a far cliff jutting out over the sea. Dawson squinted to what Joey was trying to see. It was a faded image.

"I can't tell. It looks like a woman," Dawson replied. Joey pulled Dawson's binoculars off the bench and peered through them.

"It's Kate," she replied. "She's sitting in her swim-suit all alone on the cliff," Joey observed. Dawson took a turn and peered through the binoculars. It was indeed Kate. And she looked beautiful, out on the cliff.

"She looks like a siren, straight out of *The Odyssey*," Dawson noted.

"And here I thought I was being touted as the loony one," Joey said, heading downstairs.

Dawson followed Joey. "Yeah," he said. "It's so

odd. Don't you wonder why she's doing that? At night?"

"Yoga?" responded Joey tartly. She wasn't wondering at all. She was too eager to find the Breckinridge ship, too anxious to reunite Mary with her parents, too consumed in her Lighthouse Legend. At that moment, nothing else mattered.

9

Lost at Sea

"Do you really think we'll find the Breckinridge ship?" Joey whispered to Dawson. She had reverted back to days of old and decided to spend the night at Dawson's house—one bed, two friends. It had been familiar and comforting, something Joey needed. She had woken up early but didn't want to disturb anyone. Today was the day of the dive, and she had barely slept at all. Joey looked at Dawson sleeping. She hated being the first one awake. Joey nudged him gently, trying to wake him up. Dawson rolled over. His eyes fell on Joey. Even in the morning, she was breathtaking.

"Do you think we'll find the ship today if Nick decides to schedule another dive?" she asked.

"Yeah, Joe, I really think we will," Dawson answered back, in a low voice. He was tired. Sleep hadn't come so easily for Dawson and it wasn't because of the ship. He hadn't slept in the same bed with Joey in ages. Feeling her presence beside him gave him the illusion that all was right with the world—but in Dawson Leery's world, it all wasn't right. Not just yet. A voice piped in from the floor.

"I think you'll find it, too," Jen whispered to Joey and Dawson. They had all stayed up so late talking about the legend and Mary, they'd been too tired, and scared, to go back to their respective homes.

"But what if Nick won't agree to another dive?" Joey continued to whisper, fretting.

"Then use your feminine charm," Jen murmured to Joey, softly.

Dawson grumbled, "There'll be no need for any feminine charming. Don't worry, Joe. I'll make a believer out of Nick."

"Dawson to the rescue," Jen laughed, quietly. A moment passed. Complete quiet. Then . . .

"But what if Kate won't let us take the research vessel out?" Joey continued to worry to herself, softly.

"We'll make sure she does," Dawson encouraged. A longer moment passed.

"But what if Mary de—"

"*Shut-up!*" a fourth voice yelled. It was Pacey. And he was trying to enjoy all of the one hour of sleep he'd get before the alarm rang. He was stationed across the room, his head under Dawson's desk with a blanket over it. "Can I have some peace and quiet, please?"

Dawson, Joey, and Jen looked at each other for a moment and the same instinct swept over them simultaneously. Attack! They each grabbed their pillows and hurled them at Pacey as hard as they could. He jumped, startled.

"What the—?" Pacey yelled. They made a run for it and dog-piled on top of him. "Get off me! Get off me!" Pacey kicked beneath them and eventually wormed his way out from beneath the pile. His hair was standing up straight, his T-shirt askew. He was sleep-eyed, startled, and completely disheveled. He got a mischievous look in his eye and simultaneously steam-rolled Jen and Joey, tackling them to Dawson's bed, tickling them to hysteria.

Dawson looked at his watch. "Well, since we're all up, we might as well get to work early." The tickling abruptly stopped and Pacey looked up, horrified.

"Don't you ever give it up, man?" Pacey asked.

"Gotcha!" Dawson yelled, as Pacey was bombarded with pillows for the second time. Pacey should have known better of his best friend—Dawson never ever gave up.

When Dawson and Joey arrived at the Institute, they set out to find Nick. After looking for him at the docks and in the library, they found him sitting in a wooden chair on the back porch of the Institute. Papers and maps with markings all over them were sprawled out on a bench in front of him. He had collected small rocks, which were placed on the four corners of each paper, keeping them from blowing away with the morning breeze. With a large cup of coffee, and in need of a shave, Nick looked as if he had been up all night, too. He was startled by Joey and Dawson's unexpected entrance, but relaxed when he saw it was them.

"Hey, guys," he said, yesterday's disappointment still evident in his voice. "Dawson, sorry, I should have called you this morning—I don't need your help anymore."

"Why not?" Dawson asked. "What do you mean?"

"Well," Nick explained. "It's simple. I had a set amount of time to recover the ship. Time's up. No ship. Next stop, Mystic, Connecticut." As Nick was saying it, he couldn't believe he had to give up. He should have already left but for some reason, he couldn't. He couldn't walk away from the Institute, and as much as he thought it was because of Joey, he knew it was because of something much more important to him—the sunken ship. There was something burning inside him that made him desperate to find it.

"Wait!" Joey said. She stepped in front of Dawson. "Nick, is there any way we can take out the vessel again? Today?"

Nick appreciated her dedication, but he didn't see the point. "Every time we take the research vessel out, it costs money. Money that I'm not allotted for what's now being considered a wild goose chase—"

"But what if it wasn't," Dawson interrupted. "What if we told you that we knew where the ship was?"

"What if we told you we had the coordinates?" Joey added.

Nick looked as skeptical as Dawson had when Joey told him she had met Mary Breckinridge. But Dawson persisted, and Nick was desperate to find the sunken ship. Dawson enthusiastically ran down their convincing list: the compass, the doll, the voice, the "X," the footprints, and most importantly, Dawson and Joey's charted coordinates. Nick's eyes lit up with a glimmer of hope; he was anxious to believe any information they offered him. Like Dawson, he was an optimist. He grabbed his stuff, rolling up the maps and stuffing them into his backpack.

"Come on," he said, excitedly. "Let's go." Nick jumped off the porch and headed toward the beach. Dawson and Joey were at his heels. Nick turned to them. "So, let me get this straight. We're basically taking the word of Casper the Friendly Ghost?"

"Pretty much," answered Joey. All three laughed. Nick threw his arm around Joey as they headed toward the dock, their excitement making them oblivious to the darkening sky in the far distance and the clouds moving slowly toward them.

*   *   *

Nick knocked on the door to Kate's office. "Come in," she said, as he turned the doorknob.

"Kate," Nick began his plea. "I know I've used up my time and resources in uncovering the Breckinridge vessel, but I need one more day."

Kate looked at him with pity in her eyes. She had seen a driven grad student or two in her time, but Nick was beyond driven. He was almost possessed with a need to find this ship. "Nick," she said, "I'm sorry. I can't authorize you to take out the vessel."

Nick, pleading with her, told her how groundbreaking and historical it would be to prove this legend true. He spent twenty minutes running down a list of all the information he had compiled.

Kate shook her head. "I'm sorry, Nick. The weather report is lousy. My decision is final."

Joey and Dawson waited patiently on the dock while Nick was in the Institute getting Kate's permission to take out the research vessel for another dive. Dawson had his video camera in hand, getting ready to shoot more footage. Joey stared out across the water, up at the lighthouse. Pacey had agreed to replace Joey as tour guide. Joey laughed to herself, thinking of Pacey giving tours and ad-libbing anything that came into his head. Tourists would probably leave Manor Light knowing more about Deputy Dougie's quirks than the lighthouse's historical facts. Her thoughts were interrupted when Nick ran over. He picked Joey up and spun her around. "Let's go!" he said.

Within an hour, they were headed out to sea. When they sailed out to the first orange buoy, they turned southeast. Dawson looked through his binoculars, making sure they were in line with the tree marked with the "X" on shore. The wind had picked up a bit, but Nick said it was still safe to dive. Joey hoped they would be able to spot the ship. Nick could prove there was a historical basis for the legend, Mary's spirit could join her parents, and Joey would be able to put her fears behind her. While Joey continued to think, Nick and Dawson made conversation at the helm.

"So, Nick?" Dawson asked. "Do you believe in ghosts all of the time or only when they can further your career?" Nick smiled. Dawson was all about the barbs. Nick could tell Dawson really didn't like him.

"Well . . ." Nick thought for a moment. "Since this is the first ghost I've ever encountered, I'll have to see how it goes. If we find the ship, you can count me as a believer!" Joey smiled. Like Dawson, Nick wasn't the type of guy to jump to quick judgments.

"What about you, Joey?" Nick asked. "I assume you're a firm believer?" Joey thought for a moment. A week ago, she might have said no. But today, she nodded her head.

"I believe that spirits stay with you. You can't always see them and they don't always do things as blatant as moving broken compasses or carving 'X's' into trees or papers with coordinates. But I believe they are with us, letting us know they are with us, all of the time."

Dawson looked at Joey. "How, Joe?" he asked, softly.

Joey thought for a moment. "It's little things," she said. She told Nick and Dawson about how her mom used to put little inspirational quotes in her lunch box the first day of every school year. After she died, Joey found a quote in her lunch box the following school year.

"Maybe it was an old one?" Dawson offered. Joey shook her head.

"I had never read or even heard the quote before," Joey responded. "It was new."

"Did Bessie write it?" Dawson asked, playing devil's advocate. Joey was getting upset. Why did he always doubt her? He asked her to give an example and now she was talking about something she never discussed and he was trying to prove her wrong.

"That's really beautiful, Joey," Nick said. Dawson rolled his eyes. Great, he thought, now I'm the bad guy . . . again. Joey was touched by Nick's sincerity.

"It's just little things like that," she continued. "They add up and eventually you feel like that person is there with you, every step you take." Listening to Joey, Dawson felt like a jerk. He loved when she opened up. It was so rare but it was so pure. He felt awful for acting like he didn't believe her again. Contrary to popular belief, he had grown beyond his black-and-white world. He believed in happy endings, storybook romances, and fairy tales. He valued those cheesy clichés that his grandma embroidered on little pillows for him when he was a kid: honesty is the best policy; patience is a virtue; love can conquer all. He wanted the good guy to defeat the bad guy; he wanted nice guys to finish first, not last; and he wanted to believe that soul mates always found their way back to each other. But most of all, he wanted Joey to know that he was her biggest supporter of all.

"I'm a believer, Joey," Dawson said, "and I do believe you. Something is definitely going on. Something more outrageous and scary and even magical than any plot or scenario." Joey smiled. She could tell that this time his words actually meant something.

Meanwhile, Jen and Pacey were in the aquarium trying to calm a frantic Abigail. The mother dolphin was swimming in circles around her baby.

"What is she doing?" Pacey asked.

"I don't know," Jen responded, concerned. "She's been like this for the past hour. Kate's on her way." Pacey smiled as Kate burst through the door, as if on cue.

"Kate!" Jen said. "I'm so glad you're here. I don't know what she's doing . . ."

"Abigail is sensing that a storm is coming, that's all," Kate interrupted. "I've been sensing one, too," she added.

"I was afraid she was having another baby or something," Jen joked. Kate laughed.

"No worries . . . in here, at least." Kate stood up and walked over to the window. Her gaze fell on the dock—she saw the research vessel was missing. She turned to Jen and Pacey. "Do you know where Joey and Dawson are?"

Pacey happily answered, "Something about the high seas, a sunken ship, and a buried treasure."

Kate was serious. "Pacey, did they go out on the research vessel?" she asked, sternly.

Pacey nodded. "Dawson said Nick okayed it with you. They were doing another dive." Kate looked out the window as the storm clouds moved in quickly.

"I'm calling the Coast Guard," Kate said, leaving. She turned back. "You two go to the lighthouse and turn on the light."

Pacey thought for a moment. He didn't want to seem argumentative, but he asked, "Does the light work?"

"Just go," Kate said. And with that, she was gone.

Joey lowered herself into the water; the time had come for one last dive. She was feeling the pressure of the situation, everything rested on her instincts being correct. What if they swam down to the depths of the ocean and there was no ship? What would Nick think of her? What if she couldn't help Mary? Joey closed her eyes, not wanting to have doubts.

Nick followed behind Joey and together they sank down into the sea. Deeper and deeper they swam . . . first five, ten, twenty, thirty feet. This time, Joey refused to notice any of the spectacular sea life swimming around her. All she cared about was finding the ship's wreckage. Joey swam down a little farther, to forty feet. Once she hit that point, Nick motioned for her to stop. That was deep enough for Joey. She swam around in gigantic circles, scanning the ocean floor. Nick continued.

Joey flipped around in the water. She had to find the ship. She could feel Mary's presence with her. With Mary's knowledge of the accident, Nick's meticulous research, Dawson's eventual belief, and Joey's open heart, they had all helped to take Mary to the spot of her parents' death. Joey felt like a big sister, protective of this little lost soul, who was finding her way back home to her family.

Joey looked down to check on Nick's progress below her, as he sank to sixty feet. He was swimming in circles around something. He waved his arms around and gestured an enthusiastic "thumbs up." On the ocean floor she could just make out part of a wooden ship. Joey couldn't believe it. Was it really the Breckinridge ship? Was it really in the exact spot they thought it would be? She hoped they weren't getting their hopes up only to find it was some other wreckage, from some other ship that had suffered a similar fate.

Joey watched Nick pick something up. He held it up for her to see. It was a plaque from the ship, which read *Queen Mary*. The *Queen Mary!* Joey was sure this was proof; it must have been the name of Mary's ship. Queen Mary would have been the nickname for Mary Breckinridge, too—an only child, adamant about getting her way, enthralled with Joey's made-up stories about kings and queens. They had found the wreckage! Nick was holding a piece of history in his hands. Joey wanted to pull off her equipment and throw her arms around him.

But she couldn't. Nick had given her specific instructions and Joey had a job to do. She waved and slowly swam up to the surface. She broke through the water and swam over to the research vessel. Dawson saw her and turned the camera to her.

"Well?" he asked. Joey spit the tube out of her mouth.

"We found it," she yelled, happily. "I saw part of the ship. Nick's down there with it!"

"It was really there?" Dawson asked, in disbelief.

"Yes! Can you believe it?" Joey was ecstatic. "Right where we thought it would be, Dawson," she answered. "Do you want to come under with the camera? You probably won't be able to get down to the bottom, but we can drag around and zoom it in."

Dawson acted fast and put on his wet suit. Joey climbed on board and helped Dawson with his equipment. Her face came close to his as she pulled and tightened his outfit. After a couple of minutes, he was ready.

Joey lowered herself into the water. "Can you hand me the rope? I need to bring it down to Nick." On board was a rope and pulley system used to help bring large objects up from the ocean floor. Joey needed to get one end of the rope to Nick and then come back up to the vessel to coil the handle and help pull the wreckage up. Dawson tossed Joey one end of the rope, which she quickly swam over to and grabbed. "Thanks, Dawson," she said, shoving the air tube back into her mouth and sinking under the surface of the water. Dawson, his camera strapped to his chest, quickly followed her into the water.

Nick met Joey and Dawson between the ocean floor and the surface. He gave Dawson a "thumbs up," which Dawson gave back to him. Joey handed Nick the rope and watched him sink down to the ship. Joey and Dawson started adjusting the underwater camera. Dawson was able to zoom in about ten feet from the wreckage. Nick signaled to Joey an "okay" and she pulled her end of the rope back up to the surface.

Back in the research vessel, Joey reeled in the rope. She leaned over the side of the boat, waiting to see what Nick had chosen to pull up from the wreckage. After what felt like an eternity, Joey saw something poke through the surface. Simultaneously, Nick popped up out of the water. Dawson was still filming the recovery right beneath the surface.

"What is it?" Joey asked.

Nick answered. "It's part of the mast and the boom." Joey helped Nick hoist it up over the edge of their boat. "Careful," he reminded. With Nick's help, Joey carefully pulled the piece of the ship over the side and gently set it on the deck. Next, Nick helped Dawson bring up the camera and the two joined Joey on the vessel. Nick had the broken *Queen Mary* plaque in his hand. The three stared in silence at the wreckage, amazed. For a moment, no one said a word. Finally, Nick broke the silence with a yell of joy. Joey and Dawson quickly followed suit. Nick grabbed Joey and gave her a huge bear hug and then did the same to Dawson. This wasn't about having a crush on Joey; this was about discovering what they had been searching for. Joey and Dawson embraced as well, the three of them in shock that they actually found part of Mary's ship. It had happened—the legend was reality. The mystery was solved.

Dried off and in warm clothes, their triumph was cut short when the boat suddenly lurched to one side. In the midst of celebrating, Nick, Joey, and Dawson had failed to notice what was happening around them. But reality quickly hit them. The sky had darkened and the clouds were now covering what had been an endless blue. Light mist turned to rain and within five minutes, a torrential downpour. Nick barked orders to Joey and Dawson.

"Get some rope!" he yelled. "We need to strap the mast and hull down." Joey quickly obeyed.

"Is that our first priority?" Dawson was worried. "Shouldn't we try to get back to the dock first?"

"No, no," Nick shook his head. "We need to strap this down first." He seemed more concerned about the wreckage than returning them safely to shore. Dawson knew from experience that if the waters got too rough, it would be dangerous to dock.

"Nick," Dawson yelled. "We've gotta leave."

Nick looked at Dawson and said firmly, "I'm the captain of this vessel, Dawson. You don't give orders, I do." Joey was surprised at Nick's sudden change in attitude. The three of them were supposed to be a team. "Let's go!" Nick called. "We've got work to do." Dawson and Joey quickly got to work.

Jen and Pacey entered the lighthouse on a mission. They quickly headed up the stairs to the watchtower. Unsure of where exactly to go, they both searched around for the light. Pacey went one way around the watchtower walkway, Jen went the other way. Outside, the storm raged.

Jen was the first to find the light beacon. She tried to get it to work. "Pacey," she shouted. "I found it, but it's broken!" No answer. "Pacey?"

Pacey was on the other side of the watchtower, distracted. He stared out the window, mesmerized. He squinted his eyes and looked through the rain, only to see Kate, sitting down below on the cliff, looking out toward the ocean.

"What's she doing?" Pacey wondered aloud.

Kate was drenched from the rain, her hair blowing all around her head. A large wave could roll up and knock her into the ocean, to her death. Pacey ran around the watchtower, past a harried Jen, down the stairs and out the lighthouse door.

"Pacey!" Jen screamed. "Where are you going?"

"Keep working on the light, Jen," Pacey hollered as he tossed Jen his walkie-talkie. "And double check the call Kate was supposed to place to the Coast Guard about Joey and Dawson." Jen was flustered.

"Pacey!" she called. But Pacey was out the door and gone. Jen looked out over the water and then up toward the ceiling. She tried to flip the switch again. Nothing.

"Okay, Mary Breckinridge," she said adamantly. "I need your help."

It took about fifteen visually impaired minutes to get the boom and mast securely strapped to the deck. Once that was done, Dawson, Joey, and Nick set about trying to head back to the dock. Nick took over at the helm. By that time, they had lost all sense of where they were. The white caps turned to bigger swells. The research vessel was large and not built for such conditions, making it difficult to navigate. The boat swayed from side to side, taking the rollers hard. Waves of seasickness washed over Dawson and Joey.

Joey lost her footing as one big wave crashed into the boat. Dawson reached out and grabbed the straps of her overalls, pulling her back to safety.

"Joey," Dawson screamed, over the sound of the storm. "Are you okay?"

"Dawson, thank you," Joey answered, regaining her balance. He had saved her from falling over the side. A part of her was relieved, but a bigger part was still scared to death. What happened to the peaceful ocean she fell in love with? It had turned into her angry enemy.

Suddenly, Nick shouted at them. "Are you holding down the wreckage? Don't let it get tossed around." Joey shook her head in disbelief. What about Joey getting tossed around? Nick didn't care that she almost fell overboard. He cared about his recovered wreckage. Dawson grabbed Joey's shoulders and moved her to where he was standing.

"Here," he shouted. "Stand on the inside. I'll take the outside." Dawson moved closer to the edge of the vessel, protecting Joey. The waves were swelling even larger. Nick seemed confused, lost. The winds and rain had made it impossible to navigate. Dawson shouted to him, "I think we're heading away from the dock."

"No," Nick disagreed. "This is right." The sky was so dark it was difficult to even see the approaching land. Joey grabbed onto Dawson.

"I think we're heading toward the lighthouse," Joey yelled above the screaming wind.

"Good," said Dawson. "That's close to the right spot."

Joey shook her head. "No! The rocks! There's no

way we'll be able to see the rocks until we're on top of them. Think about the legend!" Joey urged.

Dawson shouted to Nick. "Someone knows we're out here, right? Besides just our friends?" Nick looked sick and it wasn't just from the sea tossing them around. Dawson shouted again, "You did log in the research vessel's designated coordinates, didn't you?" Nick didn't answer. "You said you got permission!" Dawson fumed.

"No," Nick said, "I didn't." Nick admitted that he had lied. He had been so anxious to get out, he didn't think it would be a big problem if he just "borrowed" the research vessel. Joey looked at Dawson, her eyes wide with fear.

"No one knows our coordinates?" she asked.

Dawson shook his head and gripped the side of the boat to steady himself. Joey lurched toward him. He caught her.

"It's gonna be all right, Joe," he said, trying to convince himself. "Pacey and Jen will get help."

Joey frowned. "All they know is that we are headed southeast. They don't know our exact location."

Suddenly, a voice seemed to ring out over the storm.

"Do you hear that?" Joey screamed. Dawson listened. It sounded like someone was singing. Was it their imagination? Suddenly, the boat crashed over another wave, slamming hard into the wall of water.

"Grab a bucket," Nick yelled. Joey and Dawson grabbed plastic buckets and began scooping water out of the vessel. "I can't see," Nick screamed. "I can't tell where we are."

"We need a light to warn us," Joey said. "Without a light, we could end up just like this ship." She gestured to the recovered wreckage. Dawson was trying to be calm, but their situation was dire. It was hard enough to keep their feet on the deck, let alone find land safely.

Pacey barely made his way out to the edge of the cliff. The storm was so intense—the winds fierce, the rain beating down—he couldn't tell which way he was going. He neared the cliff, finally he was able to make out Kate's image.

"Kate!" Pacey called. She didn't move. His voice was carried out to sea by the strong winds. "Kate!" Pacey yelled again. Finally, he reached his hand out and touched her shoulder. "What are you doing?" he asked.

Kate turned, startled. "Your friends are out there," she answered. "Did you get the light to work?" she asked, not letting Pacey question her.

Pacey shook his head. "No."

"Try again," Kate demanded. "I'm very concerned. We have to save them." Pacey stared at her., frightened. Then he dashed back to the lighthouse.

Back on the water, the research vessel was being tossed about. Joey, holding on with one hand, pointed off in the distance. "I see something," she screamed. "I see a light. From the lighthouse."

"Joey," Nick screamed from the other end of the boat, "that's impossible. It hasn't worked in over one hundred years. There's no light." Another light blinked in the same spot.

"I saw it again!" Joey insisted. "We're close to the lighthouse. We're close to the rocks!" Joey continued, "It was two blinks, coming from up there," she argued with Nick. "I saw them."

Nick shook his head. "There's no way . . ."

Dawson had not seen the lights but he knew, after everything that they had been through, he could believe Joey. If Joey said there were two blinking lights, it was true.

"Listen to her, man!" Dawson yelled. Nick paid little attention. Dawson was fed up. They had risked their lives to help him and now he wouldn't listen to what they were saying. "What the hell do two blinks mean, Nick?" Dawson yelled.

"Danger!" Nick answered. "Two blinks mean danger!"

"Then turn the boat!" Joey screamed. "Turn the boat or we're gonna hit the rocks." Nick wasn't listening to her.

"Turn the boat!" Joey screamed louder. That was it! Dawson lunged over and grabbed the wheel, violently turning the vessel as they neared the rocky point jutting out into the sea. The edge of the boat grazed the rocks, causing Nick to lose his balance. He fell to the deck.

"We hit!" Dawson yelled. "We hit the rocks." He and Joey held on tight and looked over the side.

"I think we're okay," Joey said, "We just grazed. I don't think any water is coming in. The dock is right there." She pointed straight ahead as Dawson took over maneuvering the vessel from Nick. Unable to get right to the dock, Dawson beached the boat on the sand nearby. Joey and Dawson quickly hopped off, grateful to be alive and on land.

"Wait!" Nick shouted. "What about the wreckage?"

Joey turned to him. "What about the wreckage?" she screamed. "What about our lives? We could have died out there."

Dawson took off toward the lighthouse. "C'mon, Joe," Dawson urged. Joey followed him.

"Joey . . . wait!" Nick shouted after her. "Where are you going?"

"With Dawson," Joey said. "Where I belong."

Together, Joey and Dawson ran up to the lighthouse as fast as they could and burst into the door. "Jen!" Joey shouted.

"Pace!" Dawson yelled. "You guys saved our lives." Joey looked around. Pacey was nowhere to be found. The lighthouse was empty. Joey and Dawson didn't understand. Someone had guided them to shore safely. They ran up the stairs. No one was there.

They ran back outside, where the storm was starting to subside. Pacey and Jen ran up to them. "Are you guys all right?" Jen shouted, hugging Joey, then Dawson.

"Jen," Dawson called. "Did you flash the light?"

Jen shook her head. "No," she said. "I tried, but it wouldn't work. I even got so desperate I called out to the ocean and begged Mary to help me."

"Somebody flashed that light," Joey said. "Somebody guided us to shore." The foursome all had the same thought at the exact same moment. They walked to the edge of the cliff, peering over. On the beach stood Mary Breckinridge—the peaceful, angelic child Joey had grown attached to. Mary was positioned between two adults, holding each of their hands. She waved up at Dawson and Joey. Joey smiled and waved back, then looked up at the lighthouse. At that moment, one light blinked.

"Did you see that, Dawson?" Joey asked. "One blink . . . what does that mean?" They couldn't even feel the rain anymore.

Dawson watched as the little girl and her parents walked down the beach, "That means all's well."

Joey smiled broadly as Dawson put his arm around her and pulled her in close. They watched Mary walk away with her parents until they could no longer see her. Joey smiled and repeated to herself softly, "All's well."

10

The Ending

The sun had just set over the Creek. The days weren't quite as long as they had been at the beginning of the summer, but they were still long enough to fully enjoy the day. A few weeks of relaxation since their internship had ended meant lazy days swimming in the Creek, shopping in the quaint stores downtown, and anticipating what the next school year would bring. As summer came to an end, there was a feeling of moving forward, of growing up, and of moving on.

The colors in the sky faded away as Joey tied her rowboat to Dawson's dock. She walked toward Dawson's house, her hand running down the railing of the familiar wooden dock. She looked up at the ladder leading to Dawson's room. Dawson was as much her family as anyone in Capeside with the last name of Potter. He was the one constant in an otherwise unpredictable life. Without climbing the ladder, she already knew what she would find when she got to the top.

She imagined Dawson sprawled out on the bed, remote in hand, movie cued up, ready to go. Joey flicked her hair behind her shoulders as she began climbing up to Dawson's bedroom. Bessie had trimmed her hair so that it fell in an even line right below her shoulders and she looked radiant. Her cutoff jeans hung low on her hips, exposing her belly beneath her white peasant shirt. All seemed right with the world as Joey climbed up the rungs of the ladder, leading to the open window, the curtain billowing in the breeze.

Dawson was about to pop a movie into his VCR when a familiar face appeared at his window. He looked up. "Hey, Joe," he said, pleased.

"Hey, Dawson," she answered.

"Did you come for movie night?" he asked.

Joey smiled. "Depends."

"On what?"

"The theme—" Joey said suspiciously.

"What?" Dawson said innocently. "Do you think I switched genres on you and rented *The Perfect Storm* and *White Squall*?

"No lost at sea jokes, Dawson," Joey said dryly. She sat down on the bed. It creaked beneath her and she shifted to get comfortable. Dawson smiled and popped a tape into the VCR. Joey got comfortable on the bed as clambering and voices were heard out on the roof.

"You pig!" a voice shouted, followed by a slap.

Dawson peered out the window, as Jen and Pacey stumbled onto the roof. Dawson backed up to give them room as they squeezed into the open window.

"What's going on, guys?" Dawson asked.

"This cretin here," Jen said, gesturing to Pacey, "grabbed my butt while we were climbing up the ladder."

"You stopped mid-climb!" Pacey put his hands up. "Who stops mid-climb?"

Dawson eyed Pacey, knowingly. "You know, Pacey . . . you never tried to grab my butt when we were climbing up the ladder," Dawson joked.

"Funny how your hand just migrated toward me," Jen said.

"It was purely accidental, Lindley," Pacey assured her. "I want nothing to do with your butt." Joey laughed. She remembered Spring Break, when Joey yelled at him to get his butt away from hers and Pacey yelled back that his butt wanted nothing to do with her butt either. They were forced to share a bed at Aunt Gwen's house and neither slept a wink all night. But they had learned a lot about each other. Pacey learned Joey was a "cover hog" and Joey learned that Pacey wiggled his toes when he was nervous. That was a long night for both of them. Times had sure changed since then, but at least one thing remained the same—she could always count on Pacey to mildly offend someone in the room. And entertain everyone else.

"So," Jen asked. "What's going on, kids? Is movie night reinstated now that our indentured servitude is over?"

"Movie night never ended, Jen," Dawson said, as he picked up the VCR remote.

"It never ends," Pacey said, with an emphasis on the "never."

Jen looked nervous. "Please tell me it's not *Jaws*."

"Nothing scary," Dawson said to Jen. "I promise."

Joey rolled her eyes. "Where have I heard that before?" She asked, jokingly.

Dawson smiled, looking around his bedroom. His three friends settled in for the movie, Joey sprawled out on the bed, Pacey in a chair with his feet propped up, and Jen lying on the floor. They were laughing and even semi-enjoying each other's company. When you cut away the teen angst, the playful banter, the pointed insults, and the sexual tensions, it was clear what they all were to each other at the core—four best friends.

"So Dawson," Pacey said, impatient for the movie viewing, "what are we watching for our final movie night of the summer?"

"Yeah, Dawson, come on!" Jen said. "What's playing tonight?"

"Earth to Dawson! Earth to Dawson!" Joey

prompted. Dawson smiled and hit Play on his VCR.

"One Crazy Summer," he replied. "Our summer story, what else?" He settled onto the bed with Joey and they all quieted down to watch the movie.

Joey looked around the room at her three friends. As far as she was concerned, everything in her life was right at this moment. She sat surrounded by the people she loved most in the world, and Dawson Leery was by her side, where she hoped he would remain. Joey soaked in the moment. There was no question about it—all was definitely well.

The End

About the Authors

Holly Henderson has written for the hit television show "Dawson's Creek." A native of Virginia, she is a graduate of Longwood College. She currently lives in Studio City, California.

Liz Tigelaar has written for the hit show "Dawson's Creek" and also contributes creative content to its online extension, "Dawson's Desktop." A graduate of Ithaca College, she grew up in Dallas, Texas, and Guilford, Connecticut, and now lives in Santa Monica, California.